The

Eden

Virus

A Novel

By

Paul Barrieau

To my wonderful sister
I Love You

Paul

I dedicate this book to you, my first readers, in hopes that what you read here will bring you to a place you've always wanted to be.

Acknowledgements

I wish to express my gratitude to my four children; Shawn, Danielle, Caleb and Elisha. It seems that anything that I've ever done since you came into my life has been with you in heart and mind.

I want to thank my editor Linda Awana. You not only provided me with excellent editorial direction, you provided the story with content that to me, has made all the difference in the world.

Special thanks to my wife, Nikki, whose openness to the needs of this project enabled me to get it done.

To Shawn Barrieau, such an awesome job with the cover.

Finally, my gratitude to the One I cannot comprehend, but walks with me always.

FORWARD

We all know the story of the Garden of Eden from the book of Genesis in the Bible. Or do we?

Eve was tempted by the serpent, gave into the temptation and then Adam followed, making the same mistake. Their punishment was to be banished from the Garden. Or was it?

Paul Barrieau was my next door for about five years, a little over a decade ago. During that time, one of our favorite activities was to sit on my back deck, enjoy the cool Maine evening air and contemplate the world as we thought we knew it.

Paul has always been able to find meaning in things and events that others miss. His keen power of observation has always been his great gift. In The Eden Virus, his mastery in finding hidden meaning in one of the most well-known Bible stories of all time will make you pause and ask questions.

How have I read the Bible? Have I read the Bible with my own eyes or have I read it with the perspective of how it is commonly known?

The Eden Virus will encourage you to view Adam and especially Eve in a different way. It will make you re-explore what you think you know about this beloved story of our creation.

Lastly, as Paul re-examines the story of the Garden of Eden and how that outcome still affects our lives today, he has taken what we have always known and challenged our understanding. In his unique, observant way, Paul unlocks what has always been there and how that can set us free.

Ray Richardson

Westbrook, Maine

August 2015

The First Dream Filled Night

Chapter 1

A flash of bright light in the sky lit up the area in which the two were standing, and they suddenly realized that everything around them was unfamiliar. He turned back towards the entrance of their garden home but was stopped by a large ominous figure positioned at the gateway to keep him from entering. The giant figure brandished a huge shining two-edged sword, so bright it seemed to be on fire. The sound of a great boom crashed the stillness and frightened them so much they began to run away from the place they had always called home. She turned back one last time, and stopped, walking back towards the entrance instead. The figure moved aside to allow her to enter, knowing she alone could have returned but that the man could not.

The bright flash came again, immediately followed by the thundering boom. It surrounded them and for the first time in their lives they felt fear, where before, their lives had only contained peace and contentment. They knew then that they needed to find shelter. He stopped and motioned for her to quickly come with him.

They ran and as they ran, their surroundings changed from plush garden filled with fruit and vegetation to thick woods with thistles and thorns that clung to their feet and tore their skin. The mist that had kept everything in the garden moist and tender turned to a heavy rain that blinded them, increasing their fear and for the first time ever, they felt their very lives were in danger. The darkness made it nearly impossible for her to follow him. Only the flash from the sky helped her see the way as they ran for their lives.

Another blinding flash and crackling rumble and it seemed to them that the whole world was about to explode.

They were reaching the end of their strength when they happened upon a small cave cut out of the side of a mountain. There, they found shelter from the rain but not from their inner turmoil. They sat exhausted, trying to catch their breath. Staring out they watched the sky light up and reveal the forest through which they'd come. They sat, apart from each other, alone with their thoughts.

Time passed and their breathing returned to a somewhat normal rate though fear and confusion still gripped them.

She lifted her head to speak. She wanted to tell him how she felt. They had always been one with everything.

He sat in the corner of the cave, shaking his head, wondering what had happened in one day, one hour, one moment in time, a time that had had no concerns, a time in which he knew what he was doing, and now it had passed, that moment, that precious opportunity that presented itself, in which they had failed, bringing them to this place of desolation, consumed with loneliness, a strangeness they couldn't understand, a new awareness that tore them from their original identities, a knowledge of which they had to judge as truth or lie, an awareness that life will never ever be as it was when they were one with All That Existed, in harmony, secure in themselves, in love with each other, in perfect innocence, blameless in their lives because there was no knowledge, no need for it, for their relationship with all of creation was in place, intact, in harmony and now it was lost, or seemed to be, because confusion had entered their world and the lie ruled, persisted, and remained a standard by which they would measure life, love and all their actions with each other and for generations to come.

As the reality of their actions settled deep into their psyche, the awareness of its repercussions became an overwhelming thought that created a desperation and burning desire to make things right again.

"What should we do?" she said, deathly afraid to make another decision on her own, even though he played a part in their first decision. Still, she wondered how she could trust him to do the right thing ever again. She didn't understand that feeling of doubt, when for so long there was no doubt; no need to doubt. She was a part of him. They had lived by the guidance of a still small voice they could hear deep within them that now seemed deeper, smaller, and almost silent.

He raised his head and looked at her.

She felt his eyes but could not fathom what the look meant. She had never seen that look in his eyes before and she was overcome by the conflicts between love and hate, fear and comfort, bliss and confusion. She couldn't relate to these and so many other new feelings because she'd never felt them before.

She remembered the look he gave her shortly after he first saw her, the look that completed her. For so long his look gave her a sense of surety, of security. For so long, he had taken her through their world, explaining everything in detail; the beauty, awe, tranquility, perfection. For so very long his touch brought her close to him, close to her purpose, when she knew the reality of fulfillment. He was her teacher, friend and lover.

She wept.

He sat, shaking his head. He looked at her again. Gazing, his thoughts were interrupted by his observation of her appearance that he had never seen before. This view he had of her affected him differently than before. She was over there. They were apart. They had never been apart before. And once again, he felt alone and he remembered he had that feeling before she was brought to him; that feeling she had completely eliminated by her mere presence on this earth. Now everything was different. There was nothing that looked the same, felt the same and was the same. Everything was new but lacked the wonder and awe of the first newness he experienced when she came into his life.

He continued to shake his head as he bowed, looking at the dirt in the dark cave.

When confronted about what they had done, he had been the first one to speak and yet, he didn't answer either question that was posed, instead, he placed the blame on his woman. That moment was a searing pain in her heart as she remembered the accusation, betrayal and felt the bitterness of abandonment. Yet, when asked what she had done, she couldn't lie. The deception had already made its way deep into her being and she vowed then that she would put deceit out of her life.

And was it really deception; the telling of a little truth in a way intended to control the direction of thought? She wondered why she was so vulnerable to it. She wondered why she chose to believe anyone who would tell her she was imperfect or inadequate, when all that ever was, was perfect. She wondered what she would do with her life now; with this man who betrayed her -- he whom all her desires were for, whom she loved.

The cave was dark but dry. So many things were different and the cave gave them shelter from the water coming down from the sky. They had never seen such water. It had always been just a mist, and now, the skies opened with water coming down in drops as big as the tears from her eyes. There was a chill in the air and they were thankful for the robes He had given to them.

"What is coming down from the sky?" she asked not really wanting to have a conversation with him but wanting a distraction from the thoughts that were tormenting her.

"Rain", he answered, without hesitation, as he had put a name to all things in their world.

He had never seen the water come from the sky in such that way either, but her question had only interrupted his dark thoughts. It was these thoughts and feelings of hopelessness, despair and failure that had grown in his mind, destroying any memory of peace, happiness and purpose.

He then remembered the words, "you shall surely die" and at that moment, he actually hoped to die. He could see no reason to live. He remembered the Tree of Life that they were now banished from in case they should eat from it also. Now, he did not see it as punishment, but a blessing. His desire for death was so deep.

She fell asleep.

He wondered how she could sleep through all of this. How could she sleep while his *very* heart was so haunted with torment and pain?

Chapter 2

Sue awoke to the crash of distant thunder; a sound that still sent shivers of fear deep into her being. She was lying there motionless but for the quickness of her breath and the sound of her heart pounding in her ears. The dream had been so real, the fear so intense, that a light sheen of sweat appeared on her brow as she laid there, her back to him, her eyes tightly closed, trying to quiet her breathing. She heard him moan in his sleep, his breathing labored, and wondered, what was disturbing his sleep. A thought, like an intuition, flashed through her mind – somehow she felt that he was having the same dream. The thought disappeared as the next peal of thunder seemed to crash directly over their house, their room, and their bed.

Marc's eyes flashed open, adjusting to the darkness of the bedroom, still overcome with the fear and confusion lingering from the dream, enhanced by the storm raging outside. Though his back was to her, he knew that she was awake because of the sound of her breathing. She seemed troubled, afraid. He thought of turning to comfort her, but dismissed the idea immediately. The fight last night created that kind of distance. His thoughts went to the dream and he realized a distance had also been created between the man and the woman in the dream. The fight he and Sue had had before they went to bed last night was over the same things: the

boys, the schedule, the multitude of responsibilities, their careers --
all the likely targets that provided them with an escape from
confronting their real issues.

He looked at the alarm clock and realized he didn't have to
get up for another thirty minutes. He had a very busy day ahead of
him. It had been Sue's turn to take the boys to school and attend
their after school activities that would last well into the evening,
however because of a commitment at school, Sue was unable to
take them.

Marc was infuriated with Sue because she wouldn't change her
schedule. He knew she had planned for a long time to have a guest
speaker for two of her classes, which coincidentally occurred
during the boy's activities, and though he understood what a
privilege it was for her to have this particular guest speaker, inside
he still selfishly blamed her for the busy day he had before him.

The stress began to build, the more Marc thought about all
that had to be done today. On top of his duties with the boys, he
had a high level meeting at work with the executives of a company
who were considering a merger with the firm he worked for. He
laid there just wishing all of these responsibilities would go away;
he was overwhelmed and tired of them all.

Long ago, they had both agreed that one of them would
always be at the boys' activities. And though challenging, they had
been very successful at this one thing in their marriage of fourteen

years. He was uncertain why he was upset about going, when it was something they both wanted for their children. He felt a pang of selfishness but easily dismissed it.

As soon as Marc's thoughts shifted away from the dream, his mind went into full gear. He seldom experienced joy and rarely allowed himself to relax. Accomplishments only provided a small relief and very little satisfaction. He was a driven man. He was a great actor in every situation outside of the home. He had a winning smile and a countenance that exuded confidence and success. He wondered why he felt everything but that, and lived his life trapped inside of a person he felt he wasn't.

Sue was different from Marc in so many ways. While he was outgoing and charismatic, she was somewhat quiet, seemingly calm behind a mask of low self-esteem, despite her professional success. Always feeling she could be better, she looked for any way to improve herself. As a result, she was very successful and even distinguished, as a college professor and held the esteem and admiration of her peers. But her introspection seemed to limit her ability to enjoy herself. She always remembered the young, vibrant woman she was when she first met Marc. She loved how he told her of her beauty and her soft, feminine ways. Fourteen years and two kids later, now all she can see are empty eyes that stare back at her in the mirror, and she wondered why she hasn't taken better care of herself and why she felt so dreadfully alone.

And now the dream had captured her in such a way that she began a search for its meaning, hoping she could free the person she knew she was but never had been. She too was in bondage.

Before her work day even began, she had an appointment with the marriage counselor, which she did not want to miss, now more than ever. She was desperate for answers and secretly searched for a happiness and peace that she knew existed inside but somehow never let herself close to it.

It was time for Marc to wake the boys, get them ready for school and drop them off. Dealing with the boys in the morning was never a pleasant task. Seth, the oldest at 13, was slow to get moving while Morgan, 11, got up quickly like he was ready to tackle his day. Marc struggled with both of them; pushing Seth to get going with Morgan always pushing Marc. He dreaded the silent ride they had to endure each time it was his turn to drive. On the best days, the boys would be buried in their iPads and little was said. Marc didn't really know his boys and they knew little of him. He always wished he could fix that, but somehow never made the effort. Today, the ride to school would have been no different, except Marc and the boys were fixed on the storm that was raging around them. This kept the memory of the dream fresh in Marc's mind. The effects of the dream on Marc went deep. He identified with the failures of the man. He could see in him a lack of responsibility and blame towards the woman. Things he rarely admitted to seeing in himself.

Sue would usually get up in time to see her family off but on this day she stayed in bed hoping to sleep a little more, hoping the dream would continue, needing answers. She knew Marc would resent this and she always knew he would voice his resentment at the worst time. She felt a flush of guilt about wanting to stay in bed longer, but tried hard to dismiss it. She longed for more of the dream; somehow she felt it held answers, truths she needed in her life.

As soon as Marc drove off, Sue got out of bed. Sleep had eluded her. She went to the kitchen and found no coffee made, no note to her, and dirty breakfast dishes on the table, laundry piled up on the floor of the laundry room and lights left on throughout the house. With all the evidence of life and family around her, she felt more alone than ever. As the thunder continued to shake the house, she made a cup of instant coffee and sat at the kitchen table to consider her day, her marriage, her family, her dream, her life.

~~~~~~~

When Marc got to the office, there was a note on his desk from his boss, Matthew, to see him as soon as he got in. Matthew told him that Chad's wife went into labor and Chad would not be at the office today. Without Chad there, it would be on Marc's shoulders to give the presentation this morning. This gave Marc two hours to prepare. Marc saw this as his chance to "one up" Chad which would put him in the best seat to be the company's next president, a position Marc had been pursuing for some time. But whenever there was a water cooler conversation, it appeared that Chad was the favorite. Now Marc had the opportunity he was looking for.

As Marc poured over the presentation and the information that Chad had compiled, he realized the depth of understanding, intuition and ingenuity Chad possessed. In that moment he recognized Chad's qualifications for the very job he coveted. But it would be Marc that would deliver the presentation that everybody would remember, and therefore, it would be Marc that would get the credit. Marc would give Chad all of the recognition, of course, which would be interpreted as humility. He knew he could pull this off; he gloated. Then he returned to the presentation.

It was now an hour before show time for Marc. He sat in the conference room pouring over the material. He stood in front of the room practicing his delivery. Presentations were a snap for Marc. He had done so many, but this was the one that meant the most to his employer, and certainly the one that would be most scrutinized. There would be questions. There would be challenges, there would be discussions.

The sound of distant thunder brought him back to the dream, the fear and uncertainties. He hadn't told Sue that he would be doing the presentation today instead of Chad. He thought that it didn't really matter since they were on different wavelengths these days. Their relationship was mechanical, like cogs in a machine, a clock, just making time go by.

He was alone in the conference room and the felt alone in the universe.

The storm seemed to be passing but the thunder could still be heard and Marc felt a storm raging in his personal and his professional life. He was on a high and a low, at the same time.

The dream became a vivid reality again and it played in his mind throughout the rest of the day, though one point in the dream seemed to surface consistently. It was the point at which the tempter said, "You will be like God". The thought of that quote, those specific words, raised a questioning feeling deep within him and he could not seem to grasp its meaning. It made him feel strange, guilty yet hopeful.

Chapter 3

Sue sat in Dr. Boen's waiting room. She wondered what they would talk about today. There were so many things on her mind; so many unsettling feelings in her heart. Another storm was brewing to the west. She could hear faint peals of thunder and wondered if she would think of the dream every time she heard thunder.

She looked around the waiting room, the art on the walls, the stack of magazines; nothing interested her today. Her mind played and replayed the dream, and she had to catch herself before it consumed her.

Dr. Boen was in the process of finishing up with a new client. His process for new clients hadn't changed over the many years as a therapist. The initial discovery phase was fairly simple; find out why the client thought they were there. The reasons his new clients had given over the years didn't surprise him anymore. In fact, normally within minutes, he could predict what they were going to tell him. In this appointment, the client, a young married woman, was no different. She pushed him for some immediate answers. Answers to questions like: "What do I do?", "Am I crazy?", "What do you think?"

Dr. Boen had grown very accustomed to the process. The clients rarely, if ever showed him their true thoughts and feelings. They rarely would expose themselves. Many, in fact never did, and left him to find yet another therapist. He had become very disenchanted with this phase of the practice.

This day would have been no different had it not been for a dream he had had the night before. For him, the fascination of the dream was that he could see deep within the characters in it; he could see what they were thinking and feeling. He felt he actually saw the very birth of fear, confusion, doubt, distrust, betrayal, guilt, deceit and shame, and for him, the dream had ended way too soon. He wanted to see how the story developed; how they managed all those new feelings and how it affected their relationship. But the thunder had awakened him. He thought how peculiar that the thunder was such a real part of the dream and yet it woke him from it.

Booms of thunder continued over the distant hills and Dr. Boen looked at his new client, Sarah, a young girl in her late twenties, trying desperately to live her life free from the haunts of her childhood. He would soon find out that she was the oldest of three girls. Her youngest sister had required extra care since her birth, which almost always ended up on Sarah's shoulders. Her father and mother did not get along and their marriage had ended in divorce when she was in her late teens. There always seemed to be turmoil in the home, and as the oldest, she was the one to shelter her sisters from it all.

She spent most of her teen years as a surrogate mother to her sisters and never developed a sense of who she truly was. She had deep resentments towards her parents and consequently had no desire to have children of her own. Her husband understood her feelings, but struggled with the thought of never having children.

The hour had finished and as they were confirming their next appointment, another peal of thunder shook the room they were in.

"That's some storm we're having." Dr. Boen said, as his patient got up to leave.

The young woman turned as she was walking out the door and said, "Yes that thunder was even in my dream last night and woke me up this morning."

As she passed by Sue in the waiting room, she said, with a friendly smile: "You're next."

Sue smiled, not wanting to show how startled she was after overhearing the dream comment that Sarah had made to Dr. Boen.

Dr. Boen stepped to the doorway and greeted Sue, and said that he would see her in a moment or two. Sue nodded and Dr. Boen slipped back into his office, closing the door behind him and sat at his desk, allowing his puzzlement to surface now that he was alone.

As he sat there, he became faintly aware that something extraordinary was happening. Intuition told him that it was tied to the dream that it would lead to a huge revelation, though he couldn't wrap his head around it all just yet.

He had been working on a book that covered his thirty years as a therapist and had not worked on it for months. The project had started as an exciting endeavor, but over time had become a burden of sorts and it haunted him. And though this client had presented nothing new to him in the initial conversation, her mention of the dream caused him to ponder something he had never considered. He began to see that there was, in fact, a distinct pattern with his clients that he had never really noticed before, and a small sense of wonderment tugged at his curiosity.

He wanted to sit for a while and go over the notes on his book, but Sue was waiting. He put his thoughts aside and began to ponder Sue and her needs.

~~~~~~~~

Sue and Marc had been seeing Dr. Boen for about three months, alternating weeks for individual sessions, then having a session together every third week. . During their joint session the previous week, it became apparent to Dr. Boen that Sue and Marc

- 22 -

were each floundering in their own individual lives and blaming their marriage for the current difficulties and lack of fulfillment.

Their situation was no different than hundreds of other couples he had seen over his career in counseling. Like so many others, they were disillusioned, felt betrayed, fearful, and resentful, driven by guilt but also harboring a deep seeded desire for something better.

As he continued to consider the condition of his clients, another bolt of lightning followed by booming thunder lit up his office. He thought again of his dream and the condition of the couple in it. He could clearly see them in his mind's eye, running from all the comfort they had known, into the great unknown, where fear and confusion began to control them. He wondered how they could have possibly dealt with that situation.

The continuing thunder shook him from his thoughts and he realized Sue was waiting for him.

~~~~~~~

As Sarah walked to her car through the storm, her thoughts returned to the dream. She wondered where it came from, what caused it. She had not seen anything on TV that related to it. She had not been to church or read that bible story in a very long time. The only part of the dream that she was deeply drawn to in any way was the thoughts of the woman in it; wondering why she could have been so deceived and especially why she felt herself so inadequate. She related to that in every way.

She saw herself living life constantly trying to prove her value. She was young, intelligent, and driven. She came from a financially well to-do family, was given the best education, excelled at all she put her hand to. Yet she found herself desperately trying to be accepted for who she was, while also doing all she could to avoid being hurt. Her wounds always felt so fresh, so recently inflicted, so incurable. And she wondered if anybody else felt as she did. She always felt quite alone with those feelings, but after her talk with Dr. Boen and learning of how many people he had counseled over the years, she began to wonder if anybody on earth was free of those feelings. She considered all the people she knew and started to see in them glimpses of the same behavior she displayed.

~~~~~~~

Marc's clients had arrived and were waiting in the lobby for their escort to the conference room. There were seven; four women and three men. They ranged in age from twenty-seven to eighty. They were all either upper management or executive officers for their company. The chief executive officer, Harvey, had just turned eighty. He had built the company from the ground up, over 45 years ago, and this high level meeting over a potential merger went against his grain.

Marc was well aware of Harvey's position and was also aware that any movement forward in this endeavor was to Chad's credit. Chad's ability to read people was astounding. Though Marc's success was also due to this ability, he felt that Chad was authentic and could respond to people with sincerity while Marc, only in it for the hunt, found it a challenge to hide his guile at times. He knew his veneer was thin and knew how to divert people's attention away from it and on to subjects that he could control. In short, Chad was in it to find mutual benefits while Marc just wanted the kill; Marc the hunter, Chad the gatherer.

While the seven made their way to the conference room, a boom of thunder rocked the entire building and diverted Marc's attention to the man in his dream. He began to think about what the man had lost and the way in which he had lost it. He thought that the man could not have been very involved in the life of his woman nor himself to allow such a tragedy in their lives to happen. He identified with it; he hung his head. He saw the man as a follower pretending to be a leader.

The door to the conference room opened and the seven walked in shaking Marc out of his ruminations.

There were introductions, hand shaking, and small talk around the storm and Harvey voiced concern as to why Chad was not there. Marc's boss, Matthew, explained Chad's absence and Harvey accepted it with a comment of well wishes for Chad. It was obvious that Harvey was now more uncomfortable with the proceedings but acquiesced and sat down. Refreshments were served, pamphlets were passed out and the projector was turned on.

Matthew was first on the agenda to make opening remarks welcoming his guests and offering them an open invitation to view the entire company and its records. In closing, he again apologized for Chad's absence and assured them that Marc could carry the ball with ease. He said no more. Marc was hoping for accolades, but there were none. This was unsettling for Marc, but the spotlight was now on him and he shifted into his "show time" personality, something he had always been capable of doing even in the most difficult of situations.

~~~~~~~

Dr. Boen opened the door to his office and invited Sue in with a pleasant smile.

Sue returned the smile and took her usual place in the chair near where Dr. Boen would always sit. Sue liked Dr. Boen greatly. He was somewhere in his late fifties with a rich and pleasant voice and a comfortable way about him. She felt safe talking to him. His face was pleasant and his smile genuine; she felt that he actually cared about her.

The session began as usual; the polite exchange of the status of the families and work, and, of course, a mention of the passing storms. Sue was curious about Sarah, and commented on her age and asked if she was there for marriage counseling or not. Dr. Boen only said that she was new and that she was a very bright and promising young professional. Sue realized that Dr. Boen could not say anything about their session and changed the subject quickly to her morning.

She poured over her feelings of loneliness and abandonment asking what she had done so wrong to be in this situation with a man she had grown so distant from and yet still loved so much. She explained that it was beyond her to understand why she could still have these feelings for him. Dr. Boen made a halfhearted attempt at explaining her feelings always putting his explanations in question form.

"What makes you think you've done something wrong?" he asked her.

He always asked her if she thought it could be this, or that. But to this question, she had no immediate answer. Even Dr. Boen didn't realize the impact of this particular question. They both allowed it to go without being answered.

The session continued on as usual with Sue relating to Dr. Boen certain situations she and Marc were thrown into and Dr. Boen asking her how that made her feel. He saw himself always focusing on feelings and began to think that his client's feelings were more than just emotional responses; that they were actually tied to how and what the person thought. He could not put his finger on it, but he knew that this therapeutic process he had always relied on had a very poor success rate. Another flash of lightning and boom of thunder went off and the two of them paused for a moment thinking of the dream they had both had.

Dr. Boen saw that Sue got caught up in a thought and pressed her to reveal her thoughts. Sue casually told him that this morning she was awakened from a dream that had thunder and lightning in it and she was startled by the thunder that just sounded. Dr. Boen held his breath during Sue's statement, trying not to reveal that he too had the same experience. His mind went back to the dream, the passing comments Sarah had made about thunder, and now the mention of it by Sue.

He was brought back to the present when Sue began asking him about dreams.

"Dr. Boen, do you think dreams can help people understand certain things about their own behaviors?" she asked.

She wanted to know his opinion as to their meaning, purpose and personal beliefs. This was a subject that Dr. Boen had always puzzled over. He had never really felt comfortable with the textbook definitions and the hundreds of articles published on dreams in his medical journals. His discomfort was now multiplied with the revelation of Sue and himself, and maybe even Sarah having a similar dream. He was torn between a desire to dive into Sue's dream and the desire to end the session so he could ponder the events of the day that was so young.

"There are many books written about interpreting dreams. Is there something about your dream that makes you ask that question?" he responded.

She sidestepped the question and began telling Dr. Boen that her day was pulling her in so many different directions. She told him she was dealing with her marriage, her husband, her sons, her career, the special guest speaker visiting her classes, her future, the dream, but most of all, the conflict of whom she had become, who she wanted to be, and her attempts to find out if that was who she really was meant to be. Even Dr. Boen found himself a little overwhelmed by her views and situation.

Sue ended by saying how angry she was; at her husband, family, her current situation, but her anger was especially directed at Marc. Dr. Boen sat back and made a comment that seemed very casual but struck a nerve in both of them.

"Sometimes we take things too personally, especially if it comes from someone very close to us. Only you can determine that." he offered.

He went on to say that Marc probably treats everybody with certain expectations of him in the same way; that she was no different than many people in Marc's life.

Sue fired back saying, "But it is me he is doing this to!"

When Dr. Boen said, "Maybe it is just the you he perceives or expects you to be."

Sue took a long pause to consider what he had said. Thunder broke the silence and startled her once more.

They both realized that her time was up. Dr. Boen said that he wished the session was not over, but knew that Sue needed to get to school to meet her guest. Sue agreed and they set a time and date for her next appointment in two weeks which would be a joint meeting after Marc had his one-on–one with the doctor.

Sue got up to walk towards the door and turned to Dr. Boen and said, "In my dream, there was a couple who had to deal with an extremely difficult situation and I could really identify with them. I wish it could have continued. I wanted to find out how it got resolved." Dr. Boen, again speechless, nodded his head and said that he looked forward to their next meeting. He said this in earnest and Sue felt that he actually and deeply meant it. They said their goodbyes and Sue left his office through an empty waiting room.

Dr. Boen returned to his desk and swiveled his chair to look out at the storm that was still present and actively making itself known to the world. He started writing on his notepad feverishly about the dream, the day, his clients, but paused to consider the words he had said to Sue in their closing minutes. He was stuck on the words "Maybe it is just the you he perceives or expects you to be."

He wondered about Marc's actual perception of Sue. How could she ever reveal herself to him when she so often admitted that she did not know who she was herself? He pondered about the many couples he had met and in his mind, he applied the same question to each of them. He wondered how in the world any couple could have a healthy relationship when the majority of human relationships were based on false or incomplete personalities. He became enthralled with the human mind's ability to fabricate reality from perceptions. He thought about the most consistent statement his couple-clients had made over the years, "You aren't the same person that I married. You've changed."

Chapter 4

Marc had made valuable use of his time studying Chad's documents. He had found a new, deeper respect and admiration for Chad after going over the entire presentation. Chad's notes were clear and showed a deep understanding of his audience. Chad had actually noted certain points in the presentation where he expected questions to be asked, and even took a stab at who would ask them. The layout of the notes even contained directives as to whom he should be looking at when delivering certain facts and figures. When Marc read all of this, he was determined to follow Chad's notes and deliver the message as Chad intended. It guaranteed Marc success in the delivery of the presentation which would secure his position in the company. He had no problem receiving the glory that would certainly come his way.

Marc began the presentation with as much energy as he could muster. His confidence grew as the presentation went on. He saw that Chad had orchestrated a masterpiece; even to the extent of being perfectly accurate in knowing who would ask which question. Marc was half way through it and six people had asked the assumed questions. Only Harvey had stayed silent to this point, almost two hours into it. Then Matthew stepped in and offered a short break for refreshments.

As the guests left the conference room and were directed to the restrooms, Matthew pulled Marc aside.

"Marc", he said, "I want you to know that I have never seen a presentation so skillfully delivered in all of my life. You have represented the company and what it has to offer in a way that the most cynical would have to take a step back and reconsider their position. Keep it up boy, you have them, and me, completely enthralled."

Matthew patted Marc on the back and walked away before Marc could utter a word. In fact, maybe for the first time in his life, Marc was speechless.

A new flash of lightning and crash of thunder shook the room and Marc's thoughts, once again, returned to his dream. He knew the old Bible story all too well and thought about how the man had been chosen to be the caretaker of paradise and yet, in a few moments time he threw it all away, betraying the very one that was sent to be by his side. This disturbed him to his core. He did not know what to think or how to deal with the emotions these thoughts conjured up. More thunder and Marc had to quickly compose himself to become the man he had been for the last two hours.

~~~~~~~

Six of the seven clients returned to the conference room. Only Harvey remained outside the room talking with Matthew. As the door closed, Marc could see that Harvey was doing most of the talking and a couple of times pointed in Marc's direction. He wasn't sure if the gesture was directed at him or not, but it presented another challenge for him to compose and continue with the presentation. Matthew motioned to Marc to proceed and closed the door so he and Harvey could continue their conversation in the hall.

Marc flipped his internal switch, turned to his audience, put on his plastic smile; it was show-time. He easily picked up right where he left off. Marc found it second nature just to read Chad's lines which had been prepared so well. As he got to the proposed organizational chart, he realized that it was at this point that Chad had expected a question from Harvey but Harvey was still outside talking with Matthew. His eye met Sandra's, an attractive twenty seven year old up and coming senior manager, and he was relieved when she spoke up and suggested that she should see if Harvey would be in soon. She noted that this would be one of the areas that Harvey would be most interested in. They adjourned to allow Sandra to ask Harvey and Matthew if they were ready to rejoin the group.

Moments later, all three came in and took their seats. Matthew signaled for Marc to continue.

Marc backed up a few screens in the presentation and resumed. When he finished the points on the organizational chart, right on queue, Harvey asked the exact question that Chad had expected. Marc delivered a thorough and in-depth answer that seemed to affect Harvey in such a positive way that he said, "This is very good and extremely considerate. You have obviously done your research about our people and how they have contributed to our success. The organizational chart places them correctly in positions that best utilize their skills. Please continue."

Matthew looked at Marc and gave him a look that conveyed appreciation and admiration.

Marc finished the entire presentation in the time allotted him and sat down very much relieved that it was over, but also very exhilarated.

A new set of lightning and thunder added energy and excitement in the room. Nature's commotion only caused Marc's thoughts to return to the moment this morning when he awoke from the dream and the feelings of failure and desolation. When he thought about sharing news of the successful presentation with Sue his exhilaration suddenly faded and was immediately replaced with as sharp stab of loneliness. He felt certain that he and Sue would not be able to genuinely share the good news of his day. Sue's day would trump his as usual.

Matthew suggested that they all meet for dinner that night, but Marc had to opt out because of his responsibilities to his sons. Marc resented this because Seth and Morgan had never shown enough appreciation for all that that he did for them.

Matthew was not happy that Marc would not be coming; this seemed to happen frequently with Marc. He decided to give Chad a call to find out Chad's latest news. He wondered if Chad could possibly make it to dinner.

Everybody agreed to meet at an upscale business club downtown. They gathered their pamphlets, exchanged farewells, and congratulated Marc on an excellent job. Sandra and several others voiced how disappointed they were that he would not be able to join them. Marc hid his emotions well. Or so he thought he did. Harvey shook his hand and said that Chad would be very proud of him for stepping in like he did and doing such a commendable job. Marc thanked Harvey saying that if it wasn't for Chad's exhaustive work he could never have done what he did. Harvey seemed to agree, as did Matthew.

They all left the conference room and once again Marc was alone with nothing but his notes. More thunder crashed and the sense of abandonment from the dream combined with his present loneliness hit hard; Marc cursed it all from his core.

After everyone had left, Matthew returned to his office to find out that Chad had already called him to tell him his wife had delivered a healthy baby girl, their third daughter. Matthew called him back to congratulate him and tell him how the meeting went. He told Chad about the dinner engagement and asked if he would be able to attend. Chad said he could but would not be able to stay very long.

Matthew was thrilled at the answer saying, "It just wasn't the same without you here today, Chad."

Marc walked by his office, overhearing Matthew's comment to Chad. Matthew waved him in and Marc immediately became apologetic for being unable to attend the dinner.

Matthew interrupted him saying, "Don't worry about it, Chad can make it".

"You did a great job; the presentation was fantastic," smiled Matthew, "now it's time for Chad to kick in."

Marc accepted this. In a sense he was relieved and glad he wasn't going to the dinner. In a casual setting, he felt that the clients might actually see that he was not the brains behind the day. He felt that maybe it was better that he leave the situation on as high a note as possible and not ruin any positive perceptions they may have of him.

"Thanks, Matthew, I appreciate that," he said, then added "I need to run and pick up the boys now." He turned to leave as Matthew said that it was fine and that he could take tomorrow off if he so desired. Marc thanked him but said that he would be there in the morning. Days off never provided him with respite unless he had a golf outing or something to take up most of the day. Marc nodded a goodbye and turned to his office to collect his things. Matthew observed Marc's countenance and wondered why the sense of gloom.

Chapter 5

As Sue left Dr. Boen's office, her mind continued to think about the things that he said. Because of her professional background, she had been very hesitant to see a marriage counselor. Dr. Boen had been recommended to her by a friend who encouraged her to see him, even if not just for the sake of Marc and the boys. When she finally decided to go for counseling, she had an attitude of knowing more than the doctor, but in a very short time, she discovered that there were things in her that needed that kind of attention. Perhaps a different set of eyes besides hers, her friends, family and fellow professors that were close to her; the eyes and ears of a relatively disinterested third party. Today, when Dr. Boen made the comment about Marc only treating the Sue he perceived her to be, she began to wonder who that person was in Marc's life. Had she been hiding a part of herself from him that the relationship needed; that she needed? These questions could have occupied her all day long had it not been for her guest speaker.

Her thoughts then shifted to the guest that would be speaking a few hours from now, and she became excited at what he may deliver in his lecture.

~~~~~~~

Sue was Professor of Sociology at a prestigious local university. Her interest in human relationships was an integral part of her being. She could not remember a time when she did not find people and their relationships with each other and the world around them of utmost interest to her. She was raised in a religious household, attending church regularly, participating in the events and adopting the lifestyle of the congregation, but she always came away puzzled because the behavior of the congregation. Their actions outside of church were inconsistent with what she witnessed each Sunday morning. Sometimes the behavior was so vastly opposite that she felt they were hypocrites. She had left the church community some time ago. Marc was not a church goer and she used that as an excuse to leave the church.

This guest speaker, Dr. Josef Turgeon was from a quaint town on the coast of Maine by the name of Peaquod Pocket. His area of expertise was known throughout the world community of sociology. His special area of study was on the effects of religion and cults on both people and governments. He had recently published a thesis on his theories that made him a candidate for the Nobel Prize in Sociology.

Sue, more than ever before, wanted to hear him speak on his thesis. And after the dream she experienced, she could hardly wait to hear him talk. She could barely contain her curiosity and now had a million questions for him. Would he be able to address the extreme situation of the couple she had dreamed about? Would his expertise help her to process the conflicting emotions that coursed through her every time she tried to figure out what the dream could mean? What possible outcome would stay the confusion, fear and feelings of loss felt by the couple?

~~~~~~~

Dr. Turgeon's drive south to this small mid-Atlantic university town was relatively uneventful. He liked to drive when time permitted. It gave him great opportunities to reflect on his studies and experiences. He often worked with psychologists and psychiatrists to discuss their businesses. He had developed a little psycho-sociological think tank with a few of his local colleagues. They would meet regularly to discuss anything that related to their particular fields of expertise. He had one of these meetings just the day before, so he had plenty to contemplate during his relaxing five hour drive.

During the "think tank" meeting, he shared something with the team that startled all of them. He told them that the intense publicity he had received on his thesis had actually caused him to reconsider his position. The group became very quiet though he knew they had a thousand questions.

He went on to explain that some of the questions asked during a recent press conference related to his candidacy for the

Nobel Prize, were asked in a very aggressive and insulting manner. He said most of the questions asked had little effect on him. He had expected a fair share of disagreement and contention, so wasn't really surprised by them. However, one question from a reporter seemed to stand out from the rest. He had been surprised by it because the young reporter had little background, relatively speaking, compared to the community of professionals. Maybe, he thought, that is why the reporter could ask the question.

Dr. Turgeon told his colleagues, "At times, I get caught up in the science and lose sight of the simple". He smiled at his friends, then continued, "I think the reporter was free of the science, hence the ability to ask the simple and somewhat profound questions."

He told them most of the questions from the community centered on who and what he used for facts, historical and current, to support his theories. There was so much tension in the room as the words "cult" and "religion" were paired. Some even disqualified the facts that he offered so instantaneously that it was as though nothing he offered as substantiation would be accepted. But when they seemed to have come to the end of their challenges, this young, somewhat serious reporter had stepped forward. He had been there for the entire press conference, which was more of a panel discussion than a press conference. He had not said a word nor asked a question until the room grew quiet. The reporter then addressed him with genuine respect and an obvious absence of biases. The reporter seemed uncomfortable with the question he was about to ask and had difficulty phrasing it, knowing that it would surely be taken offensively by some and laughed at by others. Yet, he drew his breath and asked, in a very simple manner:

"Dr. Turgeon, I am sure you have considered this question many times, but I do not see it addressed in the thesis. So, for my sake, would you please explain the difference between a religion and a cult?" The entire room grew still.

"I looked at the reporter", said Dr. Turgeon. "And time seemed to slow down. I knew he was not looking for the age-old book definition of the two. But, considering all the flack that I had just received from the community, I made a choice; the textbook answer was the easy way out and I took it. However, I added, whether any particular group's beliefs and practices are really divergent or original makes an exact definition difficult."

"You know" he continued, "It has always been the simple questions that return to me and it has been the simple questions, not the complex ones, that have led me to reconsider my opinions. And when I'm able to let go of my pride, I have found that they often lead me to change my views. Strangely, this usually leads me to a deeper peace in my life."

One of the attendees, an older therapist, casually added, "It's amazing to me that we all find it so difficult to let go of our pride when time and time again, it always proves to be the better path to take. It's almost like facing death when confronted with changing our beliefs." He chuckled.

"What bondage we put ourselves in! Don't you agree? I mean, time and time again, we prove that our beliefs are based on just that. A belief; not facts, but beliefs, like believing in Santa Claus. And when we do change, we put all our eggs into a new basket. I don't really know what the options are; I just see our behavior and wonder why."

Dr. Turgeon continued to replay the meeting as he neared the end of his drive. He spent a lot of time thinking about the statement from The Old Therapist, "It's almost like facing death when confronted with changing our beliefs. What bondage we put ourselves in!"

Dr. Turgeon had spent some time studying the scriptures from the many religions of the world and this statement led him to think about a scripture from the Christian bible that was very similar to The Old Therapist's statement "...for fear of death, they are held in bondage."

His pondering was cut short as he signaled to enter the university campus. Though he had been driving through the storm for the last hour, he had not noticed its effects. As he drove through the campus, he marveled at some of the downed trees and scattered debris. He loved a good storm.

Chapter 6

Sarah made her way to work through unusually heavy traffic due to the storm. As the lightning and thunder continued, she couldn't help but think about her dream. The origins of man had always interested her. She often looked at the evolution of man throughout the ages and wondered why mankind is easily deceived. She held a secret belief that she felt was also held by thousands of people. She longed to meet people with like beliefs, but as of now, had not met anybody and didn't know how to.

At work she was an aggressive, detailed oriented person. Her only weakness was seeing and accepting that people are truly different from her, with different work ethics and different values. At times she actually felt that people without similar goals and drives were what caused most of society's problems. Her life was wrapped up in her work and in her status. Most of her life was managed as if it were a project. She was driven to achievement and used her material strengths to create and protect a chosen persona she felt she could maintain. All of this led her to have several broken relationships. She was very appealing, so it was easy to attract men. She quickly dismissed any suitor who wasn't success driven and she had a very narrow view of what success was.

Her young marriage caused much conflict in her. She had hoped that it would free her from the haunts in her life. She was now disappointed and confused. Her friend Kelly suggested that she see a therapist, if only to talk and hear herself talk.

Sarah was a project manager and had recently earned her Project Management Office (PMO) certification. This made her eligible for a much higher salary and as a result, she was named senior project manager for a very high visibility, extremely expensive technology upgrade for her company. She couldn't wait to get started on it. To her, it was a project manager's dream which gave her a sense of pride and fulfillment.

She and Kelly, were great friends even though they were almost polar opposites. Kelly was vivacious and charming; she had worked hard through public high school, seeking scholarships and writing essays to attract tuition dollars since her family was unable to pay for her college education. It was a huge accomplishment that she was a graduate student at Veritas University. In fact, Sarah secretly admired her friend's single-minded perseverance in the face of the many obstacles that had been in her path.

Kelly was currently taking a post-grad class in which Sue was the professor. Kelly had told Sarah about Dr. Turgeon's visit with enthusiasm because of his interest in human behavior. She told Sarah that it would be great if she could attend one of Dr. Turgeon's presentations as he is up for a Nobel Prize and how many times would she get to hear a Nobel Prize winner speak?

As Sarah drove to work, she was actually considering the invite. She had recently had a performance review. She received extremely high grades, in all areas but one; interpersonal skills. This bothered her to a point of anger as she felt that she wasn't the problem at all. Other people should do their jobs and do them according to the plan which she considered holy and unapproachable.

A sudden flash of lightning followed quickly by booming thunder caused thoughts of her dream to interrupt her rationale; she decided that maybe the content of the lecture would help her and decided to accept Kelly's invitation.

~~~~~~~

Sue arrived at her school on time and went to her first class well prepared and excited as usual. It had been easy to prepare for today's classes. She had given the students Dr. Turgeon's thesis to read for homework and the class would consist of the students responding to its contents. Her plan was to see how they would react to it before and after his visit.

Kelly was in the first class of the day and had read the thesis all the way through with a voracious appetite, yearning to learn and understand it all. She found it unique and exhilarating to read an opinion of someone with such appeal and support from the community. She even did additional research and found a transcript from the panel discussion in Switzerland. She was young, energetic and very impressionable.

While reading the transcript, however a question began to tug at her. She too noted the young reporter's question, but was taken back by the canned answer that Dr. Turgeon had given. It was an unexpected response from such a prestigious man as Dr. Turgeon. She was hoping for the opportunity to ask him if his answer was something he truly bought into.

During the class in which Kelly attended, many of the students also offered up questions as to the facts and figures that Dr. Turgeon had used for his thesis. Kelly found it absolutely interesting that nobody mentioned the reporter's question; her professor did not mentioned it either. Kelly wondered if no one else had read the transcript all the way through and decided to keep her question to herself, saving it for Dr. Turgeon in person who was scheduled to speak in just over an hour.

~~~~~~~

Seth's spring soccer league game was first on Marc's agenda. It was held in the soccer field of Midtown Middle School, where Seth attended. The boys' schools were adjacent to each other, making the day a little easier for Marc.

For Marc, soccer was as boring and un-American as a sport could be. To make matters worse, Seth, though filled with natural athletic ability, showed little fire in competitive situations; he did not seem to take the games seriously. Being a competitive sportsman, this created yet another wedge between Marc and his older son. Morgan, on the other hand, was quite the opposite, having to push himself, always working extremely hard for his place in sports; his hard work usually paid off.

The soccer game turned out to be very competitive. The teams were vying for first place and they were evenly matched. Seth played offense and actually showed some true interest in the outcome. He played with more intensity than he ordinarily did, and the game ended in sudden death overtime when Seth made a brilliant move on one of his defenders and scored the winning goal.

As Seth was mobbed by his team-mates and cheered by the fans, Marc stood on the sidelines receiving accolades from all of the parents and fans for his son's success. Marc had actually been busy doing business on his iPad and missed the winning play completely. This only fueled his deep feelings of guilt, irresponsibility and resentment towards most everything in life. But true to his persona, he showed absolute elation and pride for his son.

Morgan, always the observant one, knew that his Dad had missed the play and wondered for a moment if his Dad put on the same kind of act during his own events. And coming up next would be Morgan's championship baseball game. His focus turned back to his big brother whom he was so proud of; he looked up to him and often wished he could make Seth's life happier.

As Seth walked towards his Dad, Marc patted him on the back saying, "Well done, Seth! I guess you showed them you could play after all." Marc's words did nothing for his son and they walked together toward the car as Morgan showered praise over Seth.

More than an hour went by and the lightning had gone. The umpires for Morgan's game were meeting to determine if the game should be played. They conferred with the coaches and decided that they would start it. But if there was any more lightning they would pull the players from the field and stop the game. The umpires and coaches went over the rules covering the requirements of a game being stopped because of the weather. They went over the lineups and ground rules, shook hands and let the game begin.

Chapter 7

Dr. Boen was finishing his day early. He had a short list of clients that day and was glad to get out of the office before lunch time. It was just more of the same issues, more of the same people not willing to face their lives, more of the same people not able to enjoy life; being immersed in and holding on to their problems. He wondered why people reacted to life's situations in ways that just caused more suffering. He wondered if they really wanted change. He wondered why they chose to suffer. They all seemed to be so fearful of a different way of life saying "This is just the way I am" or "I guess this is my lot in life." He was so grateful that his work day was over. A question flitted across his mind, had the couple in the dream chosen to suffer, by the very fact that they'd believed the tempter, believed a lie? He wondered, is that why we suffer now?

Sue had invited him to Dr. Turgeon's event at the university. He had read the thesis and some of Dr. Turgeon's other documents and found him to be unusual in his perceptions and, at times, challenging. He felt that Dr. Turgeon was yet another person with deep seeded resentments towards religion, organized or not, yet he was curious about the man, if just for the courage it took to record his controversial opinions. He put his biases aside and decided to go.

Dr. Turgeon was giving two presentations that afternoon; he would attend the second one. He pulled out the notes on his book and studied them some more. His thoughts went back to his statement to Sue about how Marc viewed her. He thought about all of his clients and who they portrayed themselves to be and who their spouses perceived and expected them to be. He thought about the many times he had heard couples say that their spouse was not the person they had married. And he thought about his wife and asked himself who she saw him to be. He then challenged himself with the same question; how did he see his wife? Had he put her in a box? Had she correctly perceived what that box was? And had she acquiesced to it to keep the relationship alive? Was he doing the same with her; living up to her perceptions to keep the relationship alive? Did this bring about true happiness for couples or just relative comfort? Isn't living according to someone else's idea of the "real you" just another lie, another part of the suffering? His mind spun around this, trying to make sense of it all.

His thoughts were interrupted by the rumbling of distant thunder.

A new storm started to show itself, appearing more powerful than the first one. The lightning and thunder was ominous and foreboding. He thought of the couple in his dream and again wondered how they dealt with their relationship going forward, in light of what each of them were facing on a personal level.

With a bright flash of lightning and immediate thunder the lights in his office flickered. He looked at the clock and realized it was time to hit the road, get some lunch and head for the university. He grabbed his briefcase, and in it put a copy of the thesis and an old bible he had stuffed away in his bookcase, turned out the lights and left for his car.

~~~~~~~

After the secretary had announced his arrival, Sue stepped out of her office and greeted Dr. Turgeon with a genuine smile and a warm handshake.

"It's so nice to finally meet you in person!" she exclaimed.

He spoke slowly and precisely, "The feeling is mutual, Sue. I would recognize you anywhere by your enchanting voice." He smiled warmly.

Sue thanked him for the compliment. Actually, her voice was something she had always liked about herself; it had a high tone with a sincere feminine quality to it.

Marc had told her several times how much he liked her voice, that it was one of the things that attracted him to her. Once he mentioned how her voice was authentic, somehow the essence of her true self. Sue loved hearing those things. At that moment, she felt as though she saw a glimpse of her authentic self; it gave her a feeling of wholeness. She liked it.

"Please have a seat here, Dr. Turgeon. You must be a little frazzled from your drive." Sue said in the most accommodating manner she had, which really came natural to her.

"Why, thank you!" Dr. Turgeon said. "But please call me Joe. I feel we are already friends." he said, looking directly into her eyes.

"Okay!" Sue said feeling like all her troubles were put on hold and she was free to be herself, by his unassuming acceptance of her. Somehow she didn't feel judged; she felt liberated. And she liked the feeling immensely.

They exchanged the typical pleasantries of the day. They also gave each other a little history of how they got to be where they were in their professions.

Sue's path was very typical; an early childhood interest in human relationships followed by educational pursuits that brought her to the university. Dr. Turgeon mentioned that he had known the now deceased Dean of Sociology at the school, Dr. Reginald Kawika, and felt privileged to have known such a wonderful man. Sue agreed wholeheartedly with him. Dr. Kawika had been such a valuable friend and mentor to her before his death. She mentioned how honored she'd been to be able to read many of his written works.

Dr. Turgeon said, "Yes, I know. He had spoken to me of you in the past. He said that you were very promising protégé and also very dear to him." Sue wondered if the doctor noticed how touched she was by his remark.

"I gave your thesis to the students in two of my classes as homework this past week. I asked them to read and respond in class to its contents", Sue said.

"And what were their responses, if I may ask, to get a little head start on the lectures?"

"Well, to be honest, I was a little disappointed", Sue shared. "I had hoped that there would be some that would dig deep, wanting to know more than just the facts and figures. Instead, most of the students stayed within the confines of the ordinary. Their comments only confirmed my basic expectations." She didn't want to admit to him that she felt a sense of failure as a teacher, but as she considered revealing this, the doctor spoke up.

"Well I guess that is understandable" he said. "In fact, that is not so different from the response I received from the panel discussion held in Switzerland on the thesis."

"Really! How did that strike you?" Sue asked.

"Well, "he continued "I guess I should have expected it. I've been told by many that the thesis challenges age old paradigms on how we view cults, religions, and even government, for that matter. And that scares people. It means change and, as you know, people are afraid of change, especially when it comes to things as deep rooted and close to home as those systems.

"I guess I should have half expected it also" Sue said. "But there was this one grad student in attendance that I had hoped to get more from. Her name is Kelly and seems to have that inquisitive fire in her that we educators look for. She said nothing, which is very unusual for her."

Dr. Turgeon nodded but said nothing, understanding how people set expectations. He sat back in his chair; put his hand to his chin, posing a look of inner reflection.

"Sue," he said, "May I share something with you that came out of the panel discussion, which coincidentally was also a press conference?"

"Of course!" She said.

He went on to explain the minutes of the panel discussion and how he answered the questions from the community. He felt that each of his answers supported the fundamental beliefs that brought him to his conclusions. He told her that he never wavered during their interrogation and as the discussions came to a close, he felt surety in his thesis.

"Then a young reporter ask me a question. He asked me to explain the difference between a religion and a cult."

Dr. Turgeon watched Sue's face with interest as she tried to process the answer for herself. He then shared his own inner conflict as he battled with his answer. There was an easy answer, and there was "his" answer. He explained how he ultimately relented by giving the "acceptable" easy answer.

"But are there many other ways to answer the question he had?" Sue asked trying to make him feel like he had done nothing wrong.

"Well" he said, "for me the truth is this: I had always felt the answers I gave were appropriate and truthful, until I was forced to answer this particular question. I didn't have that much time to think about my answer. I was asked the question in a way that required me to truly consider if the clinical response was what I truly adhered to." He paused for a moment. "The fact is, the answer I gave is really not the one I believe in deep down."

He continued: "It bothers me when I hear things like: 'Well that's the way we have always done it' or 'that's what we have always believed'. And yet I still answered in a fashion that went against my grain and it disturbed me."

He paused, though she felt sure he had more to say.

"Please go on" Sue said captivated by the discussion.

"Well", Dr. Turgeon said after pausing a moment, "I think this is one of those conversations that could go on into the night and I think we only have about thirty minutes before the first lecture. Let me just say this: the young reporter's question made me rethink the definitions and the differences between religions and cults." He continued: "I heard my canned answer and compared it against my true beliefs."

He thought for a moment, then continued: "I can fairly easily define the similarities and differences, but a new question crossed my mind. Is it a certain culture that classifies a belief system as a religion or a cult? And if so, then the classifications are left in the hands of people and how they determined what is acceptable and unacceptable in each different society. If culturally defined, won't the definition and acceptability vary vastly from culture to culture, nation to nation?"

Sue sat there, attentive to every word the doctor said. But the conclusions the doctor had made were slightly outside of her grasp. It was a new way of thinking. It presented a challenge, it gave her hope, it caused her to reconsider conventions she had blindly accepted all of her life.

"I know this may sound fairly simple and maybe even quite pedestrian," the doctor added, "but these thoughts have led me to view our very existence in a different way. Now I ask myself, how much of what we humans really believe is actual truth?"

She nodded her head; too much in thought to say anything.

Sue then noticed the time and got up from her chair saying, "I guess I need to make sure all is set in the lecture room. I will leave you to prepare. I do hope we can continue this conversation soon."

The doctor rose from his chair as Sue left the office. "See you soon." He said.

As the door closed, the doctor sat back down, took out his notebook and began to write.

~~~~~~~

It was the bottom of the seventh inning and the score was tied nine all. Morgan's passion and his keen awareness of everything that was going on in the game, showed on his young face; everyone could see that his heart was in this game.

He was glad to be in the outfield where nobody could see him. He had been suppressing this overwhelming need to go pee and his failure was now showing up on his gray baseball pants. With two outs and the bases loaded, his coach called for time out to talk with the pitcher. After a moment or two on the mound, the coach signaled for Morgan to come in and pitch. He was completely unaware of the condition Morgan was in. Mortified, Morgan proceeded to the pitcher's mound. He had to focus and get the job done.

Marc was unaware his son's condition until Morgan wound up for the pitch. The first ball was thrown, it was a strike and the crowd cheered. Marc hung his head having no idea how to deal with the situation; torn between his own embarrassment and that of his son. The next three pitches were called balls and the crowd for Morgan's team booed the umpire for what they perceived as bad calls. Then Morgan threw a strike down the middle and once again the crowd was cheering for an out.

The next pitch hit the exact same spot as the previous strike, but the umpire called it a ball. Morgan had walked in the winning run.

He was destroyed and ran to the bench only to bury his face in his hands weeping uncontrollably. His best friend and teammate, Norman, sat down beside him with his arm around Morgan trying to console him. Morgan had completely forgotten about his pants and the wet disaster he had shown to the world. His only thoughts were that he had lost the game, the championship game.

Marc stood outside the dugout waiting for Morgan to appear. His stomach was tied up in a knot, commiserating with Morgan in a way he'd never be able to fully express. He had no idea what to say that could make anything better for his son. Seth stood by him, tears covering his ruddy face, for as much as they never really connected as brothers, he felt deeply about his little brother and what had just transpired. He intuitively knew that Morgan's grief was about the game and only the game, nothing else. He was so very proud of his brother.

As Morgan came out of the dugout, head hanging low as he walked toward his father. Marc came alongside and walked with Morgan. He reached out to him; he pat him on the back a couple of times, but did not know what to say. So he said nothing.

A huge flash of lighting and clash of thunder alerted everybody there that the storm had come back to life and they made their way to their cars with one team celebrating and the other wondering how they could have let this one go. Marc, Seth and Morgan got into the car and drove off in silence. A silence louder than any they had known before.

As they drove home, the thunder and lightning only reminded Marc of the dream and reinforced his feelings of failure at the things in life that mattered most. From the depth of his being, he knew that things were wrong, his relationships were shallow, and his heart hardened and closed off. His day had been a road of highs and lows and the resentments grew to a point of rendering him helpless and under the control of his emotions, a condition he loathed. His thoughts spiraled downward to the dark core of the kind of self-centeredness that made it nearly impossible to show love to another human being.

Now, he had to go home and face Sue, who would be bathing in excitement and success that was earned and appreciated. He felt so low, he wasn't sure he could stand the high she'd be on. He already resented her for it somehow.

Chapter 8

Dr. Boen had a planned lunch with an associate of his who specialized in counseling people who had gender disorientations. Dr. Boen made it a point to meet with other therapists whose area of expertise differed from his. This helped him have a broader understanding of the human psyche. He also felt that it supported his desire to be more accepting and less judgmental of others, so he pushed the envelope whenever he could.

Just as Dr. Boen arrived at the restaurant, he received a phone call from the associate apologizing for a last minute emergency and asking for a rain check. Dr. Boen assured his friend that it was not a problem and they made another lunch date for the following week. Dr. Boen went into the restaurant alone.

He was actually a little relieved at the turn of events. He felt that today was not the best day to talk with his associate, as he was pressed for time. In addition, on the ride there he had begun considering the contents of his dream again and wanted to write down more of his thoughts.

He took his seat at a booth, gave the waitress his order and as she left, took out the bible and began to read the chapter in Genesis that related to his dream.

"Now the serpent was more cunning than any beast of the field which the Lord God had made. And he said to the woman, "Has God indeed said, 'You shall not eat of every tree of the garden'?"

And the woman said to the serpent, "We may eat the fruit of the trees of the garden; but of the fruit of the tree which is in the midst of the garden, God has said, 'You shall not eat it, nor shall you touch it, lest you die.'" Genesis 3:1-3

As a young man involved in his church, he had read the story of the Garden of Eden many times, but the readings had never produced the thoughts and questions he had as he read it that day. He especially noted one passage where the woman responded to the tempter's question by saying, "God has said, *'You shall not eat it, nor shall you touch it, lest you die.'"* When he read that she said *"nor shall you touch it"* he realized that this is not what was said to the man earlier in the story: *"...but of the tree of the knowledge of good and evil you shall not eat, for in the day that you eat of it you shall surely die."* No mention of touching it. Why, he wondered?

His years of meeting with clients brought him to ask why the woman had added that; did the man misquote God to her. Did she add that on her own, and if so, why?

As he sipped his coffee, he let his thoughts ponder the possibilities. He concluded, with hesitation, that the woman must've added it on her own. She could not quote God because

God had not told her; the man had told her. She had to know that she wasn't telling the truth and that would lead to her obvious feelings of insecurity, when confronted by the serpent."

He read on and more questions started to fill his mind: "Where was her man in all of this? He was nearby yet did not speak up. Why were they near that tree? They must have known it was risky. Why did he eat from the fruit? And what is it in the human spirit that would cause us to be so weak, so susceptible?"

He thought that the tempter's words were very powerful, or was it the way they were said that made them powerful, made her doubt? They were mixed with truth and lies and they could not divide them correctly. He thought about how the woman was tricked into comparing herself to God. And in that comparison, he saw the woman felt that she fell short and was not all that she could be; she was not "like God".

The direction Dr. Boen's thoughts were taking him started to become a little overwhelming. He felt that this story of old held some truly profound insights into the human experience. A discernment so deep and primal that he longed to sequester himself in a quiet room to give it the time and attention it deserved.

However, time was passing. His meal came and he needed to finish and get to the lecture on time. He felt more inclined to hear what was to be said. He wanted to hear the questions and the answers. He felt a little as he did when he first started his pursuits into this field. He was curious and wanted to know more; he looked forward to Dr. Turgeon's lecture and hoped for more insight.

~~~~~~~

"That's awesome!" Kelly said when Sarah called to say she was going to the lecture and needed to know which room it was to be held in.

"Well" Sarah responded, "You're right! How many times will I get to hear a potential Nobel Prize winner?" Kelly gave her the name of the building and the room number.

"Oh! I have another call. I'll see you there." and Sarah hung up the phone.

Sarah then switched her phone to the incoming call. It was her husband calling to say he couldn't make it for dinner tonight. He had to work late and would see her later in the evening. She resisted responding, not wanting him to hear the hurt, which she usually disguised as irritation.

This wasn't the first time he had done this. She was beginning to feel like his job was consuming him and that he had no time for her.

She liked a man that had a drive for success, as she herself had, but she began to realize that this drive was not conducive to the kind of relationship she now wanted. These thoughts created a feeling of ambivalence. She was torn, not knowing how to manage the conflict inside of her. She set it aside in one of her mental compartments. She decided to leave it for now, but felt a little cold and empty inside. She now hoped that the lecture would provide her with a diversion from these feelings, so she prepared to go with renewed anticipation.

~~~~~~~~

Dr. Turgeon sat in Sue's office writing down some notes for the lectures. He knew that he was not facing a gathering of his peers, except for the faculty and specially invited guests. His purpose there was to direct his attention to the student body that attended and he gave that his full consideration, tailoring the lecture to suit his audience.

He remembered his days in college and how susceptible he was to new ways of thinking. He recalled how he was so easily impressed by people with high stature, those with degrees and titles, and how vulnerable he was to ideologies that touched his emotions and tickled his intellect. He believed that college was the time in a young person's life when they decided who they were or who they wanted to be. That young people are in search of an identity that they can uphold; one that helps them fit in or be in control.

He knew that his lectures would have a profound effect on these young people and he wanted it to be a positive one. More than that, he wanted to leave his audience with a license to ask questions, to think creatively and even to challenge his information if they wanted to. And even more than that, he wanted them to listen and learn to judge for themselves the merit in the answer and not judge the person who gave it.

Dr. Turgeon considered these things but felt that he was missing something very important and could not put his finger on it. He hoped that maybe it would become clearer to him during the lectures. He chuckled for a moment thinking that it was not a "piece" that was missing from the puzzle, but more of a "peace" that was missing in his thoughts.

After a few soft knocks on the door, Sue opened it and asked Dr. Turgeon if he was ready to go. He looked at her with that quiet smile, and nodding his head, got up from the chair saying, "Yes, I believe I am, Sue."

As they headed toward the lecture hall he asked: "How much time do I have before I open it up for questions?"

"How much time would you like, Joe? I'm hoping that the students are completely engaged and will have questions that show their interest and encourage you to expound. I, for one, would like that," Sue said with sincerity.

"Well," the doctor said. "Let's see how it goes."

"Sounds great to me, Joe," Sue said, just wanting to get it going.

They left the office and walked down the corridor to the auditorium, which was not that far away. As they got to the entrance, they were stopped by Sarah, who asked if this was the place that the Nobel Prize winner was speaking.

Sue and Dr. Turgeon spoke at the same time,

"Yes," said Sue.

"No," said Dr. Turgeon

They laughed and Sue said that she had found the right place and to go on in. Sarah said "Thanks", paused a moment looking at Sue, trying to place her, and went in. Sue and the doctor waited a moment and then followed through the doorway.

As Sue and the doctor walked down the center aisle to the stage and the podium, the students recognized who it was and stood giving them a welcoming ovation.

Sue walked to the podium, the doctor at her side, and addressed the student body and guests, welcoming them and introducing Dr. Turgeon. She told the students of what had just occurred at the entrance saying that her desire for the doctor to win the Nobel Prize was great and that she hoped that the student body would feel the same after today. The statement was met with smiles and applause.

Dr. Turgeon took his place at the podium and the students once again stood, giving him what seemed like a victorious ovation, though he hadn't yet begun. The doctor tried to silence his audience with thank you's while gesturing for them to take their seats.

He addressed them, "Let me begin by expressing my gratitude to Professor Ludwig for inviting me here to talk with you all. In the short time we've known each other, I already feel like we are friends." He smiled and turned to Sue and expanded, "Thank you very much, Sue."

"Professor Sue Ludwig is an excellent educator and we share a passion for sociology. I'm so grateful for the opportunity to speak with you all." Again the applause came; and again he gestured with a wave for them to let him continue.

After a moment of reflection, he began by telling the students how difficult it was for him to write the thesis. He told them how he considered the people close to him, family and friends, as he was writing it. He knew that its contents would upset some and maybe even challenge certain relationships he held very dear to him; even his immediate family. He let his gaze scan the audience, letting that information set in for a moment before continuing.

He told the students of his fears that his family would bear the brunt of some public scrutiny. That their lives could be impacted in a negative, and maybe even a dangerous way.

"In the end," he said, "I decided that the content of my thesis were just my opinions. Some of those opinions have now become true beliefs," he paused, then continued:

"I concluded that, as I have let my family live their lives, they should do the same for me. Most of all," he continued, "I decided to trust the love that we share as a family, "he said, emphasizing "trust the love".

He continued: "After all, this wouldn't be the first time they had to endure the ramblings of this old man." he said with a chuckle.

The crowd laughed at that and again applauded. He hoped that they perceived the message that they should live their own lives and especially to "trust love". This was a message he felt the younger generation needed to get ahold of.

He had never used that phrase before and as he pondered it, he felt it merited more thought; he quickly wrote a note to himself to revisit it later.

Sarah sat in the audience; her heart stopped beating for a moment. She was touched by the way he chose to trust love. It gave her hope. She knew she needed this kind of trust in her life as well, that it would bring sensibility to her hectic and fractured lifestyle.

The applause subsided and the doctor continued speaking. He did not go into a lot of specifics within the thesis. He instead spent a large amount of time talking about his approach, the external challenges and how he met them; the wide range of responses that he received from the community and the affects those opinions had on him, even to the extent of making him question his own opinions. He mentioned how people can be so easily swayed by the opinions of others.

He explained that there were those who wanted to "stone him" and those who wanted to make him a saint. And through it all he tried to stay neutral without accusation toward anyone.

He then jumped into the subject that mattered most to him. He talked about how the challenges from the sociology community were so strong, it caused him to deeply consider the true source of their concerns. He said that there were those who objected to how closely he related cults to religions. They all seemed to be protecting something.

"This only made me feel like they had an agenda of their own." He continued: "I found it difficult not to disqualify their opinions and objections on the basis of conflicts of interest."

He looked around the room to see if the audience was following him. He saw Sue in the front row; she was fixed on his every word.

He cleared his throat and continued, "There were also many that wanted to discount the importance of my statements in the thesis related to the effects that religion and cults have on government." The room went quiet; the audience almost motionless.

"Personally, I can easily substitute the word 'people' for 'government'." He said, then continued:

"People reason that religion is a part of the fabric of society and that the obvious influences, both good and bad, have always been considered as a natural phenomenon, therefore accepted as normal."

He paused briefly to survey the audience. There was very little movement in the room, all eyes seemed to be on him.

He continued by saying that he had arrived at a place in his life where he could not accept those reasoning's anymore. That he, in fact, challenged what the accepted "normal" was.

"To put it bluntly," he said, "I looked at the condition of our world and concluded that it just wasn't working. We still have war, poverty, hunger and despair. Yet, it is these conditions that both religion and government have always said they want to end. At this point, it appears to me that they may be the cause and not the cure."

Many of the students stood and began to applaud. He motioned for them to end the applause and return to their seats. It made him very uncomfortable. He knew he had just made a direct accusation against religion and government. He decided this was not the time or place to point fingers.

The audience quieted and the doctor continued; "I must apologize for my last statement. I want you to know that I don't really believe that religion and government created those problems, but they are definitely not providing the solution. 'For the very things I hear them preach they do not themselves do.'" He quoted from scripture. There were nods in the audience and again many stood up and applauded, increasing his discomfort.

He did not want to stir up emotions. He had only hoped that each person there would consider these things on their own, and draw their own conclusions. His hope was that they would live with conviction and integrity. He turned to Sue, the smile absent from his aged face, and she only applauded along with all in attendance. For a moment, he wondered if she fully understood.

As the crowd quieted, the doctor took a deep breath and leaned into the mic saying, "I now find myself in a position that I had not desired nor planned on. I did not come here to place blame or to stir up sentiment. You see," he continued, "I really believe that many of you have felt this way about religion and government also. I am not the first to feel, think or say it. "

He let that sink in for a moment, then continued: "Please, please consider this: you all have the voice of truth speaking deep within you and it is of utmost importance that you find a way to hear it while you are young, and don't wait until you are an old codger like me." This time he did not chuckle.

Sarah hung on his words, the "voice of truth" speaking within her. She felt he was right in his observations; she very much wanted the world to change. She had a glimmer of insight into what the real problem could be, and this made her feel hopeful.

"Professor Ludwig has informed me that many of you were given my thesis to read for homework. I'm more interested in hearing what you have to say and what your questions are at this point."

He continued, "In a moment I will open up the mic for questions but first, let me comment: as to this great prize that I may or may not get, there are more times than not that I wished I was not considered for it. Please, don't get me wrong," he said, "I feel deeply honored by it all, but for me it just isn't necessary."

Before turning away from the mic, he said: "Thank you for your time and the opportunity to meet with such a wonderful and beautiful group of people. It is most certainly I who should be applauding you."

With that, he took a step back, turned to Sue and nodded for her to come forward. As Sue responded to his calling, the audience stood and gave the doctor what he felt was the warmest applause of the day.

"Well, Dr. Turgeon, this is not what I had expected from you today and I am so glad you didn't fill my expectations." She gave him a warm smile and continued, "Instead, I feel you have encouraged me and hopefully everyone here today."

"I was particularly touched when you said you decided to trust the love in your family. And then when you mentioned the voice of truth deep within us, I mean, wow, that is something I will really want to spend some time on."

She turned to the audience and said "I hope you all feel the same." They applauded a resounding agreement. "We have about twenty minutes remaining for questioning. There is a mic in the center aisle for those who wish to step forward with questions for our honored guest".

One by one, students came forward to the mic. The first few students each thanked the doctor for his words of encouragement and asked questions about his youth, his current work and his plan for the future. One even asked if he ever considered running for national office. The doctor answered each question with what seemed to him to be canned answers though emphasized that he would never run for national office.

When Sue saw Kelly step up to the mic, she said: "Kelly, I'm not surprised that you have come forward with a question," and gave her a big smile and encouraging laugh.

Kelly started to speak, stopped, cleared her throat and finally continued, as though working through her initial nervousness.

"Dr. Turgeon," she began, "I'm very happy that you visited us today. I am also very encouraged by your exhortations." The doctor nodded his head in appreciation and Kelly continued. "I, like most everybody else here, have read your thesis with great interest. But I also read the transcript from the panel discussion you had in Zurich."

She took out a copy of the transcript and continued "I want to ask you something related to the question posed by a reporter near the end of the Zurich event." Kelly paused; Dr. Turgeon nodded for her to continue.

"He asked you to give him your understanding; actually he asked you what you believed to be the difference between a cult and a religion," she stated. "Your answer confused me. It made me think that you didn't give him the answer that he wanted. I don't know if you did not have the time to answer him or that you did not want to open the proverbial 'can of worms', but you gave him an answer that came from a norm that I find hard to accept. Can you tell us what you were thinking at that time, and, after what you've just told us, would you have a different answer today?" With that, Kelly stood back from the mic to hear his answer.

Sue glanced at the doctor with a look that said, "I told you that you might get a good one from her."

Dr. Turgeon paused a moment, then looked up saying, "Your kind professor told me that she had hoped to get a zinger from the crowd today." He turned to her and said, "I hope you're happy now, Susan." Sue smiled and nodded emphatically.

He turned to Kelly, gave her one of his warmest smiles and began to answer. "I think I heard many questions from you, all packaged together, and I want to try and answer the one that means most to you." He continued, "I guess the best way I can succeed at this is to put myself in your shoes for a moment if I can."

He started by pointing out that the differences between cults and religions, as well as his opinion of them, were secondary. Kelly nodded. "I think what you really want to know is 'why did I cave in' Yes?" Kelly nodded again with a sheepish grin.

"Well to be honest, I did cave in." He said, apologetically.

"Because I believe that different cultures have their own definition of what a cult is, at times I find it difficult to see if there is a difference at all. I knew this statement would cause controversy at the conference and I just didn't want to tackle the issue at that time." he explained, realizing he began to feel a sense of freedom by voicing this.

"Kelly? That is your name?" Kelly nodded. "So, yes, I took the backdoor. Let me also add this, and I hope that everyone here can understand and accept it: I have learned and am still learning, to listen to that still, small voice I hear when confronted with something that just doesn't set right. And when I recognize it early enough and pursue its prodding, I find that it leads me to truth." he paused.

"If I may quote one that I consider to be among the very few enlightened ones of all time who said: *"...and the truth will set you free."*

With that, the doctor started to step away from the mic, the "still small voice" telling him it was not over yet. He smiled to himself.

Kelly, not entirely satisfied, quickly asked: "Doctor, may I ask then what are we set free from?"

Dr. Turgeon glanced over at Sue with his kind smile, then turned back to Kelly and said, "Lies, Kelly. We are set free from any lies we have believed. I believe this is what leads to true freedom in life."

Kelly spoke up again, "What lies, Doctor?" she asked in a quizzical voice, one that seemed to be searching for her own personal freedom.

"Well, Kelly, that is the question you all have to answer for yourselves. And if you are willing to hear the truth and have the courage, conviction and integrity to let it have its way in your life, then you will discover what lies you have believed. But this courage I mention is paramount because at times you will feel like you are facing death itself."

She nodded her head, somehow understanding this, even though she was so young.

As the doctor said these words, he remembered what The Old Therapist had said the last time they were together: 'It's almost like facing death when confronted with changing our beliefs...'

He looked out at the young audience and silently prayed for them to have the necessary courage.

He then stepped back and Sue came to the mic. "Well" she began, "I think Dr. Turgeon gave us some deep things to consider. I know that this is true for me, I hope it is the same for everybody here." She turned to the doctor and said, "Thank you Dr. Turgeon for your time, your candidness and especially your challenging words."

With that, Sue adjourned the event and the audience rose with an applause of appreciation.

~~~~~~~

After the games were finished, Marc and the boys picked up a pizza and headed home.

There was no conversation; each kept to his own thoughts. Lightning and thunder heralded the beginning of another storm, as powerful as the one that woke him in the morning. The thunder stirred up the dream which made him confused and left him feeling like he fell short in so many aspects of his life. He wanted to say something meaningful to his boys; what he thought they needed to hear from him. Being so wrapped up in his own pain, he couldn't think of a thing to say. So he said nothing.

When they got home, they headed straight for the kitchen and started in on the pizza.

Marc reached over for a slice of pizza and reminded them that he was going to visit their grandmother in the nursing home and would be gone for about two hours. He told them that their mother should be home soon.

As he was walking out the door, he turned to the boys and in a voice that he had used before, he said with sincerity, "Morgan, Seth, I want you to know that you should be proud of yourselves today. I know I am proud of you." They lifted their heads in unison, looked at each other and then looked at Marc saying a simple "Thanks, Dad." Then Morgan added, "Say Hi to Grammie for us!"

Marc walked out the door and went to his car. His feelings were mixed, but he knew that he had spoken a truth to his sons. He *was* proud of them. It may have been the first time he had ever said that, and even more, the first time he ever really felt it. He just wasn't sure whether they truly received it or had just shrugged it off.

~~~~~~~

Marc arrived at Shady Elm Manor, where his mom lived. As usual, the lobby, was sprinkled with wheelchairs inhabited by residents of the home. Some were bent over in a position held forever, and some were looking up at him as he walked by.

One old man looked up at Marc and said, "Hello young man! How is your day going?" and held out his hand to Marc. Marc took his hand to shake and said, "Just fine, Mr. Beardsley. How is yours?"

Marc knew Mr. Beardsley from conversations with his mother. Mr. B, as everyone called him, was about 96 years old. He had worked on Wall Street as a public relations executive in a very large financial firm. He and his wife had lived at the home for two years when she had suddenly passed away. That was six years ago.

They had no children and only one niece who would visit twice a year from New Hampshire. The people of the home were his only family.

While his wife was alive, they were very active residents of the home and helped in any way that they could. But since her death, Mr. B had grown more and more solitary. So it was a rare occasion to see him in the lobby.

"Here to see your mother?" Mr. B asked. Marc said yes and that it had been awhile since he had seen her and was sure to get an earful from her.

"Oh, I don't think she will waste her time with you over that. She will just enjoy the time she has with you. That's the kind of person she is, you know?" Mr. B said, still holding Marc's hand.

Marc nodded his head; Mr. B was right. Marc patted him on the back and left for his mother's room.

Down the hall, he passed one of the nurses who recognized him and said, "Hi Marc. Boy, your mother will be glad to see you. She always talks about you with such pride and joy." Marc smiled on the outside and grimaced inside thinking, "what reason does she have to be proud of me?" And his mind continued in a downward spiral.

Marc's time with his mother began no differently than any of the other times he visited her. She had a million questions about the boys, Sue, his work and other family members. They played cribbage, which was something his mother thoroughly enjoyed. She said that it was a good way to have conversations; always filling in the quiet times in the card game.

They continued to play, as always, with intermittent small talk and game talk. Verbal jousting was always a part of the game they enjoyed, however, today there was none of the usual light teasing or competitiveness. These small things did not go unnoticed by his mother.

At one point, she looked at him with a sincere face and asked him if he still was struggling with those feelings about his father. The question startled him out of his melancholia.

She added, "You know Marc, I think he loved you too much and was afraid to get close to you."

Marc shrugged his shoulders and said in a rather cold way, "Well, all that is past, Mum. Can't do anything about it now, right? I mean I am a grown man now. I let go of all that a long time ago." He knew she wasn't fooled by the statement.

"Oh no, Marc!" his mother quickly replied. "You're still carrying it. It's easy to see it." Her face took on a sad seriousness. She began telling him about his father's early life, stories he'd heard a hundred times over.

"He's dead now," his mother added, "and you act like he is still alive." she continued, "Marc, and he did the best he could do. The very best! It may not have been perfect, it may not have even been good, but it was his best; all that he was capable of doing and you need to forgive him and let it go."

Marc threw his cards on the table and looked at his mother in a very stern way. "What is forgiveness anyway? I mean, how can I forget it all?" he said, head hanging down and really wanting an answer that would make things different. How do you let go of the feelings of rejection, he thought?

Marc's mother then set her cards down and looked at him in her loving and motherly way, her voice touching a nerve deep within, "Why do you dislike yourself so much, Son?"

He could not look at her, but continued to look at the table while seeing nothing.

"Why do you subject yourself to the hurt suffered by that little boy that is no longer?" she continued. "You yourself said that you are a grown man now. Why then do you still act like that little boy? Forgiveness is not designed to let the offender off the hook; forgiveness is to let yourself off the hook!"

She paused briefly, wondering if any of this was sinking in. She's tried so many times to help him see this; really see it.

"You have continued to live your life as a wounded person by choice and I can't for the life of me understand why. Do you really see yourself to be a wounded person? Do you see that it's really you holding onto the past, keeping it alive? Why do you punish yourself so? It wasn't your fault. Since you can believe whatever you want to believe, why do you choose to believe something that just isn't true?"

He continued to sit there without moving or responding.

After a moment she added, "Marc, do you want to keep on living that way?"

Marc hung his head even lower and tears began to well up in his eyes. There was nothing he could say in rebuttal. His mother was right. He knew it, but was still unwilling to let go of the past. He refused to let the tears spill over.

A crash of lightning and immediate thunder broke the silence and startled them both. His mother looked at him with a half-smile on her face and said, "I had a dream last night. And in it was a storm much like this one." Marc sat upright, curiosity peaked, waiting for her next words.

She continued: "In the dream, I saw a couple who had experienced a terrifying event. They seemed to be running from the safe and familiar, into a scary and uncertain future. They reminded me of you and Sue."

Marc wanted to tell her that he had had a similar dream, but suddenly he felt a little out of control of the moment. A million questions inundated his thoughts. Questions about his father, his wife, all of his relationships, his insecurities and fears -- were they all somehow tied to the dream? He desperately wanted her to continue; he didn't realize he was holding his breath.

He heard himself exhale as she began to speak: "What struck me most about this couple was the lie they believed about themselves and how much trouble it caused them. I think it is the same for you. The lies you believe about yourself have caused you more problems than can be imagined." She said.

Marc looked at his mother, knowing he couldn't hide the questions written on his face.

"Do you know what I think these lies are?" she asked gently, knowing his inner turmoil.

Without waiting for an answer, she continued: "The biggest lie you believe is that you are not good enough just as you are. "

There was no visible response from Marc, though he was so tense he thought his chest might explode.

"So many people live their lives trying to fulfill other people's expectations of them and they don't truly know what the expectations are! It's sad, because in the end, many relationships are not built upon truth, but upon perceptions and expectations."

"You may be right, Mum. You may be right." Marc admitted, though he struggled to reconcile reality with the dream. The man in the dream seemed just as uncertain and afraid as he himself was. He had expectations of the woman who was both a friend and a stranger at the same time. He expected her to follow him without hesitation and was crushed when she considered staying in the garden. It was just too much to figure out.

A nurse appeared at the door saying that visiting hours were up and that she had to prepare Marc's mother for bed.

"That is what I dislike most about my condition." Marc's mother said with a gentle sigh. "I would stay up all night talking if I could, but I know that I would pay for it tomorrow. Still, I am not really complaining. I've had my time and it was a good life filled with wonderful moments which I am so grateful for. Even my time here is good." She said. "I love you Marc and am so very proud of you."

Marc heard those words and remembered he had said the same thing to his boys just an hour before. He hoped most of all that they felt as good as he did when those words were spoken.

"Goodnight, Mum! I'll see you again soon." Marc said, and kissed her on the forehead. His mother looked up at him, returning her patented love smile. They embraced and he left the room.

As he walked slowly down the hallway pondering all she had said, he passed Mr. Beardsley's room. He looked in and the old man was sitting in a chair looking out the window into the night. Mr. Beardsley seemed so alone that Marc wished he had more time so he could go in and sit for a while with the old man.

Instead, given the hour, he walked to his car, opened the door and sat inside lost in thought and turmoil. He was so deep in thought that even the lightning and thunder couldn't interrupt.

~~~~~~~

As Dr. Turgeon concluded the second presentation, he realized it had lacked the energy of the first session. The audience seemed to be disengaged, or maybe he just perceived it that way. Was he the one that was disengaged, he wondered? No one had challenged him as Kelly had in the first meeting.　He was still quite preoccupied with the question Kelly raised. Maybe that was the problem, he thought.

At the end of the session, Dr. Boen walked away feeling a little empty handed and somewhat disappointed. However, one statement that Dr. Turgeon made did have an impact on him: "You all have the voice of truth speaking deep within you and it is of utmost importance that you find a way to hear it…" Admittedly, his attention was still on the dream and the possibility that Sue and Sarah may have had the same dream. He knew there was a truth in his dream; he desperately wanted to find a way to hear it.

When the lecture finished, Dr. Boen slipped out a side door and went home.

It had been prearranged that Dr. Turgeon and a few of Sue's colleagues would return to her office for refreshments following the lecture. She now wished she could be alone with Dr. Turgeon to continue the conversation they were having before the presentations. He told her he wanted to drive home and sleep in his own bed that night.

"Your bed becomes a very good friend as you get older," he shared. "I hate for it to sleep alone" he added with that smile of kindness.

After refreshments were served and Dr. Turgeon spent some time mingling with the guests, he announced that it was time for him to leave.

"Let me walk you to your car, Joe" Sue said. Using his first name in front of her colleagues made her feel good. They got their things together and bid farewell to those present and left for the parking lot.

As they walked, Sue turned to the doctor and said, "Joe, I cannot help but think that you have uncovered lies that you have believed and that somehow your life has changed because of those discoveries. How did the change come about? I mean, its one thing to discover that you have been believing a lie, but another thing to have your whole world change because of it. I need to know so much more."

He was pensive for a moment, then began to speak, "It depends on the lie that you have discovered within. The effects of a lie can have long lasting consequences. One who grows up believing that they are stupid may purposely pass up some of life's great opportunities because of the lie they believe. They may grow old developing a lifestyle that conforms to that falsehood. In other words, they have a faith in that lie; and faith can be very powerful."

He paused to gather his thoughts, "I am sure you noticed that I quoted Jesus in the lecture?" Sue nodded.

"Well, He also said, 'be it done unto you according to your faith.' That is a statement of the power of faith and you can see that it is true just by looking into the lives of everyday people. I also believe that if you put your faith in a lie, it will also 'be done' according this belief." Sue was silent for a moment, but his words stirred something inside her; she wasn't sure what it was. Quickly her thoughts went to the woman in her dream. She remembered how the woman was deceived by the serpent. She started asking herself what lies she had put her faith in.

Her attention was drawn back to Dr. Turgeon, as he shifted his briefcase to the other hand. He said, "If you ask people about the condition of their life they will almost always say something like, "this is just my lot in life'. But I say, 'be it done unto you according to your faith!' They may not realize what they're doing, but in their hearts, where faith is active, they believe those things. And if you believe it, the very lie will become a truth to you."

With a quizzical look, Sue asked: "Where does it all begin?"

Dr. Turgeon stopped and turn to her, looking directly into her eyes, "It begins by calling a lie a lie. That, in itself, is the 'truth that sets you free'."

They arrived at the doctor's car just as the lightning and thunder picked up again and rain began to fall. "It's going to be a great ride home. I just love storms, don't you?" he said, looking at the sky then turning to Sue at his door.

Sue said, "Well, sometimes I do, just not the kind that are a part of my life and relationships." She smiled.

"Yes," the doctor said, "and the challenge is to weather them". Sue nodded but said nothing.

The rain began in earnest. "I wish you the best and I hope to talk with you again soon." Dr. Turgeon said. He settled himself in the car, buckled his seatbelt and eased the car out of the parking stall. Sue wished they could've spent more time together; he is an intriguing man, she thought.

Sue waved and smiled as the doctor drove off.

As she stood there with the rain increasing, her mind was filled with all that had happened in her day; her dream, her time with Dr. Boen, the two lectures and the last few minutes she had with Dr. Turgeon that seemed to help her make more sense of her day.

As the lightning flashed out, she remembered that Marc was going to visit his mother; she needed to get home to be with the boys.

~~~~~~~

When Sue arrived home, she found both boys in Morgan's room playing one of Morgan's video games. This was not a typical scene; Seth seldom played his brother's games, saying they are "baby" games. Yet here he was, enjoying one with his brother.

"Hi guys!" Sue said. "How was your day? Tell me about your games?" Sue felt somewhat bad that she was not there for Morgan's big game. She rarely, if ever, missed one. They had talked a few days ago and he understood the importance of his mother's day. He was a very understanding boy, even at age eleven.

"Seth kicked the winning goal today, Mom. It was awesome!" Morgan said with enthusiasm.

"Congratulations, kiddo! I knew you could do it!"

"How about your game, Buddy?" Sue asked turning to Morgan.

"We lost." Morgan said simply without going into the details.

"Oh! I'm sorry! How did you do?" Sue continued.

"I got a couple of hits and then walked in the winning run," Morgan replied, while keeping his eyes on Seth.

"He did great, Mom," Seth quickly added.

The boys seemed intent on getting back to their game so she turned to leave them saying she was starving. Seth told her that they had pizza for dinner and there was some in the oven for her. Sue was not surprised that Marc bought pizza again.

She ate a slice of pizza alone in the kitchen while her mind went over the events of the day. She thought the presentations were both very successful and Dr. Turgeon gave everybody many things to think about. Her day had been so fulfilling yet she was exhausted.

By the time Marc got home, the boys were asleep and Sue had almost finished preparing for bed. Neither of them looked forward to their time alone. They both had had a remarkable day, yet for so long they seemed unable to verbally share anything of significance with each other.

"Hey," Marc said as he entered their bedroom; he strained to sound as though he was happy to see her. And he was, though in a somewhat distant way.

"Hi," she said, stepping out of the bathroom. "How is your mother doing?" She really liked her mother in law, but she knew Marc would not offer much information. Why wouldn't he talk to her, she always wondered?

"Mum doesn't change much." Marc said. "Always seeing the silver lining no matter what is going on in her life." He added, wishing he were the same and knowing Sue did too.

As Sue was about to respond to Marc's comment about his mother, Marc said "How were the lectures? Were they all you wanted them to be?"

Sue was caught between wanting to give Marc a lot of detail, showing her excitement or just giving him the facts and figures. She opted for a mix of the two.

"Well, Dr. Turgeon was fantastic. He is a wonderful speaker and I can easily see why he got a nomination." She said. "How was your day?"

"It was okay." Marc did not really want to get into his day in detail. There was too much to talk about; the dream, the presentation, his mother. So he steered her back to her day.

"Did any of the students ask any good questions?

"Not really," Sue said, sensing he wasn't really interested.

"Not even Kelly?" Marc asked. Sue was surprised that Marc remembered about Kelly.

Sue's response to Marc was daring in her estimation. She went into a level of detail she wouldn't normally go into with him. She even told him about the doctor's comments around the bible verse he had quoted, 'and the truth will set you free'. Sue felt Marc's questions opened a door for her to slide some things into the conversation that she really wanted Marc to hear for himself.

"Wow!" Marc said, "That's some pretty heavy stuff. Did you feel like you were in a church?" Marc regretted the question the moment he said it.

"Well I guess I wouldn't know that anymore, it has been so long since I was in a church." She wished she hadn't said it even though she felt there was no positive response to Marc's question anyway.

The room grew silent, except for the shuffling of their feet as they put clothes away and tried not to bump into each other. The silence lasted until a flash of lightning lit the room, followed closely by booming thunder.

"Man, when is this all gonna end?" Marc asked referring to the storm.

There was a long pregnant pause and Sue decided to continue the conversation; maybe this time it would help them to communicate, something she desperately wished for. She asked: "Didn't you have a big meeting today or something?"

"Yeah! We did. Chad's wife delivered a baby girl this morning and he couldn't make it, so I had to fill in for him." Marc gave her an answer that had several topics in it wondering which one she would choose for him to expound on.

"Another girl? Wow! That makes three for them right?" Sue asked.

"Yep!" Marc said.

"And how did Matt deal with the change in plans?" Sue asked.

"I guess he just had no choice but to give it to me. He told me afterward that I did well and invited me to dinner with everybody at the Brentmoor. I told him I had commitments and couldn't make it, which I am sure he didn't like at all. He called Chad who said he could make it for just the dinner."

He decided to get the topic off of himself. "Did the boys tell you about their games?" Marc asked.

"Yes, they did. Too bad about Morgan's game. Wow! The Brentwood. You must have really dazzled them." Sue continued, hoping beyond hope that he would keep talking to her.

"Too bad about Morgan's game?" Marc thought, feeling like she didn't really understand what Morgan had gone through. He didn't know that the boys never mentioned the details to her.

Lightning lit up the room again. Sue was in her pajamas, ones she didn't consider sexy, but to Marc, she looked fabulous. He wondered why he never really told her how good she looked, and silently bashed himself for the lack.

"I'm exhausted." Marc said, going to the bathroom to take a shower. Sue took that as notice that the conversation was over. She watched him go to the bathroom, slipped into bed and wondered how she would ever fall asleep, hearing the storm sounds overhead, remembering the thrilling events of the day and thinking about the conversation with Dr. Turgeon just before he left.

Marc came out of the shower about thirty minutes later, looked at Sue and concluded that she was already fast asleep.

As Marc slipped into bed he also wondered how he could ever fall asleep. His mind was racing with the thoughts of his day while the storm sounded overhead. He wondered why she hadn't mentioned her visit with Dr. Boen. He was relieved that their conversation was short and that he didn't have to listen to it.

They lay there, motionless, alone with their thoughts. And all was quiet, save for the thunder and lightning.

Chapter 9

A week went by. Marc and Sue settled back into their routines of work followed by the boys' activities. They were as distant as ever; their sleep had been dreamless. The storms had passed and the dream began to fade with time.

There had been a message in the dream, Sue was sure, but she struggled to hold on to it. She didn't realize it, but Marc had the same thoughts and feelings.

It was an ordinary day; it was Sue's turn to take the boys to school. She tried to curb her impatience and growing irritation toward Marc on this issue. Even though the school was on Marc's way to work, he still insisted that she take her turn driving the boys. He didn't seem to care that she had to go well out of her way and deal with heavy traffic, often making her arrive late to work. This fed the resentment she had towards Marc; it was only one of the many selfish and careless acts he brought to the marriage. She caught herself frowning and took a deep breath, trying to make the best of it.

Today was Marc's turn to see Dr. Boen. The truth was that Marc would rather take the boys to school than see Dr. Boen, but he had agreed to the appointment and was bound to it.

Another storm was brewing in the west and as they prepared to leave the house a bolt of lightning lit up their world and a boom of thunder shattered the silence in their life's routine. They looked at each other and wondered again about their dream, still unaware they had had the same dream. Such was their lack of communication.

Marc patted each boy on the back, wishing each a good day. He turned to Sue and gave her the usual cold hug and dry kiss saying "See you tonight".

Sue responded automatically with "Have a nice day." They each got into their cars and drove off in same direction.

Sue wondered what went wrong; how did the relationship become so lifeless and unfulfilling? The sound of thunder brought her back to the vision of the woman in the dream, out of breath and frightened, sitting in a cave staring at a man who had become a stranger to her. Once again she felt the dream had purpose and a message for her; she sometimes caught herself looking at Marc and lamenting over the fact that her husband had become a stranger to her over the years. She related to the woman in the dream. She became determined to find meaning behind the dream.

~~~~~~~

Dr. Boen got up at his usual early hour. His wife, Natalie was still asleep, her short hair in disarray around her; he thought there was never a time that she was not beautiful. He slipped quietly out of their room and drank in the solitude of their home. He enjoyed his early morning ritual of making his special omelet, coffee and a blueberry muffin. He also spent time in his study preparing for the clients he would see in his day.

Seated in his study at an old oak desk that he refinished himself, he opened his daily planner to find that his first client would be Marc. A boom of thunder shook the room and his thoughts were brought back to his dream. He took out the old bible he had in his bookcase and returned to the passage he had read in the diner the week before.

He continued on to Chapter 4 in the book of Genesis. He noticed that there was a huge gap in the time from when the man and the woman left the garden in Chapter 3, to the beginning of Chapter 4, where they had birthed their first child. He remembered how the relationship between the man and the woman in the dream had been shattered. He pondered this point, wondering how they could have rebuilt their relationship well enough to have a family. He became convinced that there were answers in these chapters that could be applied to humanity. He was determined to find them.

Dr. Boen always held that ancient writings, such as the Old Testament, held glimpses of human behavior that he saw day in and day out in his practice. He remembered thinking of his dream;

in it, he felt he saw the actual origin of fear, deceit and insecurity. There was so much there to process that he became overwhelmed; his thoughts going off in a thousand directions. Just yesterday, he decided to seek out opinions from colleagues and friends to help him find other ways to look at his perceptions. He hoped they could get together soon to discuss all of this. The whirlwind of insights was very distracting.

Another bolt of lightning lit up his study, interrupting his thoughts. He saw that it was time to leave for work so he finished packing his briefcase, headed out to the car and got on his way.

The ride to work was typical; excessive traffic and so much time spent sitting and waiting. Long ago, he decided he would listen to different radio stations along his way just to hear differing perspectives of the news. Today, he tuned to an AM station that provided a politically conservative point of view. It was a talk show and the host was talking about how America had left the intent of the founding fathers and had become a country set apart from its constitutional roots. The topic was so common on this station that he found himself only half listening. The program then cut to several commercials which penetrated his thoughts and disturbed him in a way he had never experienced before.

The first commercial offered a trip to Israel and an opportunity to visit the sacred sites of Christianity. The pitch-man talked about how experiencing the "holy land" was well worth the price and even mentioned that spiritual enlightenment could certainly be attained just walking where Jesus had walked. What disturbed Dr. Boen the most was when the voice on the radio inferred that 'nobody should pass up this chance to "grow in the Lord"'. He felt slightly irritated by this tactic, as though one had to go to the Holy Land to improve their relationship with God.

Dr. Boen had always been one to examine words and phrases used to entice people. He was fascinated by this. He thought that the ad on the radio actually used the same tactic the serpent used on Eve, essentially saying: "you could be better...if..." He thought this suggested that you are not good enough just as you are; such a disturbing message, and so easily believed by so many.

The commercial went on to say how the traveler would return from their trip better equipped to minister to those in need. Dr. Boen knew that this "promise" would entice hundreds, maybe thousands, to embark on such a trip. He also knew that this kind of experience was never necessary to "better equip you" or help you "grow in the Lord". The voice of the proverbial serpent continued to whisper, even today. He shook his head, astonished that people could be lured in by this kind of predatorial tactic. He wasn't surprised; he saw it every day in his practice.

Right after the "Israel" commercial came an ad geared towards the purchase of gold, letting the listener know how much security one would get from investing in an age old commodity. It was laced with talk of economic peril, suggesting fear for the future. It even provided a quote from Jesus when He said, "Make friends with the sons of mammon". Fear, he thought, so contagious, so debilitating. He understood how easy it was to grab onto this sense of insecurity that the media continually threw at people. He himself felt the pull of the ads even though he understood the tactics they were using.

He reached over and turned the radio off, having had enough of the negative suggestions coming from it. He thought it peculiar how these ad campaigns deduced that our society was filled with those who equated spirituality with the experience felt by visiting other lands; that it was a worthwhile pursuit to establish oneself as qualified to "minister" through expensive travel; that people can easily be swayed by well-presented commercial messages, leading to fear and investments in such things as gold; that security, stature and happiness can be attained through the offerings from an AM radio commercial. He wondered how many people actually believed the messages and realized that the answer was "many" or there would be no commercials. He thought how frail humanity is to be susceptible to such suggestions. He wondered how people could actually choose to live in such fear.

Why do we listen to words that stir up a sense of fear, of insecurity, of lack?

"These are just suggestions", he thought, but they have become truth to those who believe in them. Then he remembered that Dr. Turgeon had quoted Jesus as saying "Be it done unto you according to your faith". He realized more and more that the power of faith was enormous. And people actually *believe* those ads, he mused.

He turned into his office parking lot, got out of his car and walked in to find Marc already waiting for him. He apologized for being a little late. Marc was actually glad for the extra time he had to contemplate their visit.

~~~~~~~

After his trip to Sue's college, Dr. Turgeon had returned home without incident, enjoying the long drive. He was always glad to be home and enjoyed a great sleep in his own bed.

He settled in to his morning routine. He began each day by paying homage to his late wife, Kitty. They had established a wonderful morning ritual in their years together and he deemed it as holy ground, not to be touched or changed. It was something that had kept them close together and now she was gone.

It was taking him some time to allow the healing to take place; he missed her so much. The holy ground had been violated by her death and for months he struggled with feelings that he could not reconcile within himself. She was his soulmate, someone who helped and advised and stood by his side. Sometimes he just couldn't bear to be without her. She was so much a part of him.

It wasn't until he finished the first real draft of his thesis that he was able to begin to grasp what had been holding him in such a low and lonely existence. He had given the draft to his mentor, an older gentleman who was simply called "The Old Therapist". They had met by chance, shortly after he moved to Pequod Pocket. He remembered the occasion vividly: a Packer game on TV at the local diner, the two of them vocal about their support of the team. It naturally lead to introductions and grew into an enduring relationship.

He asked The Old Therapist for some honest feedback on the manuscript he had given him and got more than what he'd bargained for. It wasn't so much the feedback on the thesis that The Old Therapist gave him as it was the content of the conversations that ensued.

The Old Therapist had read the thesis several times before the two met to discuss it. At first, he approached it from a professional and theological perspective. He thought that the thesis was accurate in its contents and extremely well delivered; he told Dr. Turgeon as much. Even more so, he felt that Dr. Turgeon successfully mapped a way for people to be ever more free in their beliefs and the ways in which they lived out their beliefs.

The Old Therapist was very aware of Dr. Turgeon's loss and the grief it had caused him. He too had lived through several deep losses in life and it had taken some time to finally see a way to free himself from their oppressive effects. He saw the grief and wanted very much to help the doctor work through it.

He discovered that he and Dr. Turgeon had an important thing in common. He began to see that within the thesis was a cry for help from the author. It seemed to him that Dr. Turgeon was imprisoned in the same thought life that he, himself had been held captive for so long. The doctor had always shown himself to be one who dealt with such grief in healthy and realistic ways. But The Old Therapist discovered that this was but a façade and realized that Dr. Turgeon was living his life hiding his pain with nobility and practicality. He wanted to help him find the truth that would set him free.

Today was to be their first meeting to discuss the thesis. The Old Therapist pondered how he could attend to Dr. Turgeon and his real needs. He had grown very fond of the doctor, and this new awareness initiated a deep desire to bring his friend out of a darkness and into a truth. A truth he knew to be the source of living a life of peace and contentment; a life filled with adventure, happiness and love.

~~~~~~~

Marc settled into the same stuffed leather chair that all of Dr. Boen's clients had sat in over the many years he practiced. Marc wondered how many disastrous stories Dr. Boen had heard in his lifetime; and wondered more if his story was just another song sung a million times.

Dr. Boen settled into his familiar chair and greeted Marc with a smile. They exchanged pleasantries for a few minutes and though this was a typical necessity to begin their session, they both felt how empty it all sounded.

A fleeting thought passed through Dr. Boen's mind: he wondered if Marc felt insignificant, like just another of the many clients who had sat in that same chair. His intuition told him that Marc, and for that matter, anybody who sat in that chair, eventually begins to feel like just another number.

He was desperate to discover something new. This feeling was a direct result of his dream and the many thoughts he had had about it since he was awakened by the thunder and lightning. He began to wonder if the people and events in his life were all tied together somehow. He wondered what piece of the puzzle Marc might hold, if any.

After the few moments of cordial words, Dr. Boen turned to Marc and said, "Marc, I want to be very candid with you. I want to share something with you that I have never shared with any of my previous clients."

Marc sat up in his chair and with a smirk on his face responded with, "Whoa there, Doc! I'm the one here for therapy right?" Dr. Boen chuckled and agreed.

"I've been in practice for a very long time. I wonder sometimes if I have become so habitual in my methods that I fail to help my clients dig deep enough. I wonder if I take my clients for granted, assume I know the story, and because of this, possibly miss some important details."

He went on to say that he believed that Marc may have many of the same challenges. "I believe that your years in sales and public relations have exposed you to the same stories, day in and day out. I just wonder if you perceive me to be similar to you."

Marc sat up straight, and with a little curiosity said, "Yes, I feel the same about my clients and I sometimes wonder if I am just "old hat" to you. I figure you have ready-made answers to solve all of my problems and challenges." His tone was challenging, though he still felt this meeting was a waste of his time.

Dr. Boen responded by saying, "Up until the night before my last appointment with Sue, I would have confessed that as a truth." He continued, "But, the night before Sue came in, I had a dream."

Immediately, when Marc heard this, his ears perked up.

Dr. Boen continued. "The dream was so profound for me, that I started seeing my clients differently."

Marc wanted to talk about the dream, but instead asked, "So, how differently do you see me, Doc?"

Dr. Boen sat back for a moment, obviously trying to find the correct words to relate his thoughts to Marc in a non-threatening way.

"I guess," He continued, "it's not actually my perception of who you are that matters. What matters most is who you perceive yourself to be, and why."

"So," Marc drew the word out, "Is that your question for me today? Who do I perceive myself to be?"

Dr. Boen, raised his hand, pointed at Marc and said, "That's a good point, let's start there Marc, and see where it goes. How does that sound?"

Marc's body language spoke volumes to the doctor. Marc had been sitting upright completely involved in the conversation. He had especially shown a high interest with his body when the doctor mentioned the dream, but now, he started to sag in the stuffed chair and the chair seemed to be ready for that sort of posture as if all the people before him had molded the chair through the years of sessions.

Then Marc sat up a little saying, "Okay! I'm game. After all, what have I got to lose?"

Dr. Boen smiled saying that Marc's question was excellent and that his attitude just might bring about some of the answers they were looking for.

As Marc began to talk, Dr. Boen listened intently also noting the body language Marc used to convey his thoughts.

As Marc continued, Dr. Boen saw that Marc saw himself through people's expectations of him. He began by talking about his father and as he spoke of him, he slumped back into his chair. He went on to describe his mother and his body sat up a little only to return to the slump as he finished with his mother and went on to his relationship with Sue.

Marc talked a lot. He mentioned siblings, coaches, teachers, bosses, co-workers, priests, scoutmasters, girlfriends, team-mates and his school mates. When he was about finished, Dr. Boen asked him about his sons. At that question, Marc's voice became soft and withdrawn.

He thought for a moment then said, "I wish I knew how my sons saw me."

At that, a peal of lightning and thunder rang out startling the two of them. Dr. Boen looked at the clock and cursed under his breath that their time together had flown by.

"Marc" he said. "You have spent most of our time talking about how others perceive or expect you to be. You did not answer the question; not once did you say anything about who *you* perceive yourself to be. Does that tell you anything?"

Marc's head went low. He knew what the doctor was getting at and it created a fear in him that he had known time and time again. He lifted his head, looked intently at the doctor, and said that it told him something that he had known forever, but had never known what to do with it.

With a voice slightly shaken, he said "What do I do with this, Doc?"

Dr. Boen looked at Marc and with eyes he hoped conveyed deep sincerity, told Marc that if he was to tell him what to do, then the cycle would continue. He said, "Marc, the important thing here is this, what do you intend to do with this information?"

Marc looked at Dr. Boen and actually cracked an "I'm impressed" smile at the doctor. "You're good Doc. I think our time is up." Dr. Boen noted the change in Marc's countenance.

With that, Dr. Boen stood up saying that next week the three of them would meet. He said that he hoped that in the following week Marc would consider what they talked about.

Marc nodded his head and said as he walked out the door, "Maybe someday you will tell me what your dream was about." Dr. Boen nodded and Marc walked out through the waiting room where Sarah had been sitting, waiting for her appointment. They smiled at each other and Marc walked out.

~~~~~~~

Sue pulled into the school parking lot to drop Seth and Morgan off. As she was bidding them each a great day, she noticed Morgan's baseball coach talking to his son Norman and decided to catch him and thank him for all the work he had put into the season.

"Warren!" she called out and waved him over to the car.

She pulled into a parking stall and got out of her car as he came over. She conveyed her gratitude and congratulations for a great season. Warren accepted her kind words and asked how Morgan was doing since his experience in the championship game.

"Oh, he took it like he normally does," she smiled. She told Warren how proud of him she was; how he learned all that he could and then was able to move on.

"It takes a lot of character from a kid his age to be able to move on from such an embarrassing event", Warren stated earnestly.

Sue said: "It was just another game to him. You know he always seems to see the good side of life."

Warren nodded, adding "Not many kids could endure what Morgan endured that day, though."

This caught Sue's attention and she suddenly suspected that there may be more to the story than she had previously thought. She pressed Warren for more details. Warren told her the whole story.

Sue's heart sank deep within her. She had no idea that her boy had lived through such an ordeal. She wondered how he could have kept this from her. She assumed Marc had known; how could he have kept this from her? Her heart sank even deeper; she felt so disconnected from her son's life, her family and her marriage. Her emotions went from sorrow to anger to regret, guilt, pride for her son and shame in herself. She felt a deep sense of failure as a mother and a wife. She hit rock bottom.

It was hard to get her emotions under control, but she managed to thank Warren for his time and all that he had done for her son. Warren reassured her that Morgan was on the right track and she should hold on to that truth. Sue thanked him again, got into her car and sat there for a moment, trying to compose herself before heading to work. There was an ache in her heart that she just couldn't shake.

She recalled the boys recounting the events of the day to her; they were acting a little out of character that day. Why did she not see the signs that there was something beyond their words?

Something they couldn't or wouldn't tell her? Perhaps they felt it wasn't safe to share with her? Did they think that she was disinterested? The downward emotional spiral continued.

As she headed out of the parking lot, she remembered Dr. Boen saying that Marc only treated her as the person he saw her to be. As tears welled up in her eyes, she wondered to what degree this same philosophy impacted her boys. She didn't fully understand the whole theory but she was sure they were simply trying to live out her expectations of them. She didn't want that. Not for her boys.

Sue drove on, filled with thoughts and questions. There were no answers, only a lingering emptiness inside.

Lightning and thunder broke her train of thought and she again wondered about her dream.

Her thoughts went from the dream to Dr. Boen, then to Dr. Turgeon and finally settled on the girl in Dr. Boen's office who had mentioned having a dream. Something, some intuition made her feel these three could help clarify things somehow. She didn't know why.

She wondered how that girl got mixed up in her stream of thought. The girl's remark about waking up to thunder in her dream now had her attention. She also remembered that the same girl coming out of Dr. Boen's office had stopped her in the hall at school, asking for directions to Dr. Turgeon's lecture.

She recalled that Kelly and that same girl were walking together and talking after one of Dr. Turgeon's sessions. "What a coincidence" she thought, or was it more than a coincidence?

Thunder and lightning boomed out again and she began to realize even more that the dream had purpose and intent; she was determined to find out its meaning and place in her life.

As she drove on, she was stopped by a policeman in the road. He told her that there was a big accident up ahead and that she would need to seek an alternate route. She turned around and drove a few blocks in the opposite direction only to find another traffic jam. Frustrated with this development, she took a side road and came to a small intersection. She noticed a coffee shop on the corner and decided to stop in and wait it out a little. She called in to work to let them know she would be late and entered the shop. In a sense, she was glad for this interruption as it now gave her time to sit and consider all the events that had already happened in her day.

~~~~~~~

Sarah woke up early and felt as if she had gotten no sleep at all. She and her husband had argued the night before and the fight had settled into her mind and emotions, refusing to let go. It was over the same things and both lay awake till the early hours pondering on the thoughts dangerous to relationships.

She got up before him and quickly prepared for her day at work leaving her husband without coffee or a note. She decided that since she had an appointment with Dr. Boen that morning she would go to her favorite spot for some breakfast. The Half Way Café was only two blocks away so she decided to walk there. As soon as she set out she realized it was a good choice for the neighborhood streets were gridlocked with traffic jams.

Sarah walked into the café and proceeded immediately to her favorite seat, hoping it was available. It was situated in the side corner and had a window view. She liked it because she could watch life go by and also life come in for a coffee break. As she made her way toward the back, she saw that the table was already taken. A woman sat there going through the menu. Sarah was briefly disappointed but turned and began looking around for another spot. At that moment Sue looked up from the menu and saw a young woman looking around for a place to sit. Since the café was somewhat crowded due to the traffic jam, Sue tried to catch her attention.

"Excuse me! Miss?" Sue said towards Sarah who didn't seem to hear her.

"Miss?" Sue said a little louder, standing from her chair and waving her hand. This caught Sarah's attention and she turned her finger inward towards herself asking, "Me?"

"Yes!" Sue said nodding her head and waving her over to the seat opposite her in the booth. "You can share this booth with me. I don't mind." Sue continued.

Sarah smiled and looked at Sue with a quizzical look that said 'do I know you?' Sarah walked towards the booth. Sue smiled at her saying that the traffic jam had held people up, making the café crowded. "And besides" Sue said, "you look familiar. Have we ever met?"

Sarah looked at Sue, not wanting to give in right away that she recognized Sue immediately as the same woman who was in Dr. Boen's waiting room and at Dr. Turgeon's lecture. But she abandoned those cautious feelings and came right out and said that she recognized Sue as the woman in both places.

Sue could only place Sarah at Dr. Turgeon's event. She did not have a good look at her in Dr. Boen's office, but when Sarah mentioned it, she immediately realized she was the woman at the office that had startled her with her comment about being awakened by thunder in an unusual dream. She sat up straighter, her curiosity peaked. She had wanted to ask her about the contents of the dream that seemed to be similar to her own; maybe now she would have a chance.

They chatted a little about the chance encounters now numbering three, and then Sarah mentioned how much she liked this café. It was simple chit-chat to break the ice. Sue edged a little closer to her question by asking Sarah how she ended up at Dr. Turgeon's lecture. "I have never seen you in my classes or on campus before" she added.

Sarah told her of her friendship with Kelly and that the invitation to attend came from her.

"I really didn't want to go when Kelly first mentioned it. But when Kelly asked me how many times I would get to hear a Nobel Prize winner, I guess that kinda did it for me. Besides," she added "another friend advised me that it would be good for me to mix some things up in my life." Sarah was alluding to Dr. Boen who always encouraged his clients to do something that they have never done before; be it go to an opera or ride a horse or take a lesson in something completely not themselves.

"Doctor... um, my friend always has good suggestions like that." Sarah said knowing she slipped a little and hoping that Sue did not catch it.

That was not the case though; Sue caught the slip immediately and wondered how she could use it to talk about the dream comment she had overheard in Dr. Boen's waiting room.

They both started talking at the same time but Sarah dominated, wanting to steer far away from the slip if she could. "And what is your connection with Dr. Turgeon? Do you work with him in some way?" was Sarah's next question.

"Work with him?" Sue started. "How I wish I did. No! Actually, the previous dean of the university knew Dr. Turgeon and that's how he got connected to the university."

Sue eased the conversation in a slightly new direction. "And what did you think of the lectures and especially your friend Kelly's question?" she asked, genuinely wanting Sarah's answers to those questions, though she wanted to talk about other things before it was too late.

"Well, to be honest, they both blew me away." Sarah said.

Sue nodded, "I agree, the lecture was phenomenal. What parts impacted you the most?"

"Well, when he said 'trust the love', I realized what a timely message that was for me, how I needed to hear that at this time in my life." Sue listened intently.

Sarah continued, "He also mentioned the 'voice of truth'. I know that I hear it and wondered then why I seem to ignore it!" Sarah smiled and shrugged, for some reason Sue made her feel completely at ease.

Sue was intrigued with Sarah's insights and though she would have loved to continue along this line, she really wanted to ask HER question.

"The real crazy thing" Sarah continued, "was that as I was leaving the lecture I actually ran into my friend, the one who suggested that I experience something I've never experienced before. In fact," Sarah said, "I was on my way to visit with him when I got caught in this traffic jam. I hope it lets up so I can see him. He is such a busy man." She hoped Sue would not see through the ruse.

At that point, Sue started putting two and two together and took the opportunity to say what she wanted to say.

She began, "I never really believed that chance encounters had any more to them than pure chance, until recently." She added, "Meeting you today challenges those convictions about chance encounters even more." She smiled at Sarah.

"Something has stayed with me since our encounter at Dr. Boen's office last week. And here we are, yet another chance encounter! I'm glad for it because it gives me the opportunity to ask you a question."

"You have wanted to ask ME a question for over a week now?" Sarah said in the most surprising yet reserved and cautious tone she had.

"Yes!" Sue said. "I remember sitting in Dr. Boen's waiting room that morning. You were with him before me. I remember you opening the door and saying something about a dream you had and that the thunder in the dream woke you up."

Sarah was intrigued by the mention of the dream, but she restrained herself from showing any physical reaction to it.

Sue continued. "The reason I wanted to talk with you is because the previous evening I also had a deep and disturbing dream filled with thunder and lightning. It woke me and I found thunder and lightning all around me in reality. I will never forget the feeling and I cannot hear thunder or see lighting now without thinking about that dream."

Sarah was absolutely glued to Sue's words now, her heart was pumping and her hands were starting to clench in excitement.

Sue continued, "I wanted to know what your dream was about."

Sarah hadn't told anybody about her dream and she was absolutely filled with wonder and awe as to where this was all going. She decided to throw caution to the wind. She felt that Sue had been earnest and candid with her; she would be the same. She wondered if Sue had shared her dream with Dr. Boen. She took a deep breath, ready to begin, just as the waitress appeared with the bill and asked that if they were finished. Seeing the long line at the door, Sarah and Sue understood but wished they weren't so rushed.

Sarah said, "Well, we don't have a lot of time. I will tell you what I can in the time we have and if you want to, we'll meet again. We can exchange numbers and email addresses if you'd like. How does that sound?"

"Perfect" Sue said.

Sarah told Sue that her dream was straight out of the bible. "Do you know the story of Adam and Eve?" Sarah asked.

"Yes, I do" Sue said.

As Sarah related bits of the dream, Sue realized that this was not a thing to rush through.

"Sarah!" Sue said. "I believe I may have had the exact same dream! Let's definitely meet up again."

Sarah was feeling like a child on a new adventure filled with big questions and hopefully big answers.

"This is really incredible," Sarah said. They exchanged information and made their way to the door. Sarah turned to Sue as they headed their own way and said, "I'm headed to Dr. Boen's office now."

Sue said with reserve, "My husband is there now with him. We have sought Dr. Boen out for some help with our relationship."

"This has been extraordinary." Sarah said. "I look forward to our next time."

Sue nodded a true agreement and they went on their way; their minds dazed and wondering what the possible significance could be.

~~~~~~~

Sarah hurried into Dr. Boen's waiting room, running a couple of minutes late for her appointment. As she entered, a gentleman was leaving Dr. Boen's office and she heard him say to the doctor: "Maybe someday you will tell me exactly what your dream was about".

Sarah could hardly breathe after hearing the dream comment to Dr. Boen. She managed to smile as Marc passed her; Sue had told her that Marc would be there. Her heart was racing and she had to compose herself before going in to see the doctor.

Dr. Boen came to the door and greeted Sarah telling her would be just a minute or two; that he had to make one phone call which wouldn't take long.

Sarah was grateful for the moment given; she needed to get her thoughts in line with her purpose there.

Dr. Boen went back into his office to return a phone call for the therapist who had cancelled lunch with him the week previous. They set a new date and ended their phone call.

Dr. Boen leaned back in his chair and went through his normal routine to clear his head of the last appointment and prepare for the next. As he finished his routine, a bolt of lightning lit up his office and thunder clapped almost within a second after the lightning. This not only startled the doctor because of its nearness, it immediately reminded him of his dream. He was so shaken that he had to sit back for a moment. Then he remembered that his next client had a thunder filled dream. He wondered how he could lead her into talking about the dream without interrupting her or changing the natural course of their conversation. He had no idea that it was the very thing she wanted to talk about. He reminded himself that this time was for his patient and turned his focus on to Sarah, reviewing her file briefly before summoning her from the waiting room.

Sarah's hands were still holding tightly to the armchair she was sitting in. The lightning and thunder set her mind to spinning. And when the doctor opened the door, she actually didn't notice him until he said "Hello, Sarah." Sarah quickly turned her head toward him and let out a sigh saying she got lost in the moment; that the thunder had startled her.

"Yup! That was quite the bang. It sent me for a loop too. Come on in." Dr. Boen said in his always soothing voice.

Sarah walked into the doctor's office and sat in that always comfortable stuffed leather chair. They exchanged their usual pleasantries; catching up on any events they could talk about to break the ice which took all of five minutes.

Sarah started by saying that this was the second week in a row that the day had been so full that there was more to talk about than could be contained in a single session. She smiled a half smile.

Dr. Boen was not surprised by this. He had discovered that many of his clients consistently felt that way. He observed that the anticipation of an hour in the chair would usually raise his client's emotions to new heights. They were apt to be sensitive to some of the slightest things; magnifying them until they became a central point in their lives. He usually tried to work through this heightened emotional state in search of the real source of any insecurities. Sometimes he was successful, but more often than not, he did not make much headway. This led him to wonder whether people really want to be healed or if they just liked the drama.

He asked Sarah, "What is affecting you the most? Let's start there."

She didn't know how to begin. She wanted to talk about Sue. She wanted to talk about Marc's dream comment. She wanted to talk about her own dream; about Dr. Turgeon, about anything and everything that would help her make some sense of what life was presenting to her, both in and outside of the dream.

The doctor looked at Sarah sitting in that stuffed leather chair. She had the same manner and posture that she had when she was in the waiting room. She appeared to be deeply thoughtful, almost frightened, somehow curious, and definitely distracted.

"I want to take a chance on something, Sarah." The doctor said, leaning slightly forward as he addressed her. She sat up straighter, her intuition telling her something was about to change.

"When you were leaving our last visit, you said that there was lightning and thunder in a dream you had the prior evening. You also stated that it woke you from the dream."

She realized she was holding her breath as she waited for him to go on.

"I'd like to know if the lightning and thunder we just had brought something to your attention. I ask that because you still seem a little distracted by it."

A flash of lightning again lit up the room; a pregnant pause and then the booming thunder opened their eyes to another pending storm much like the one a week ago.

She took a deep breath and began.

She told the doctor about the entire dream speaking so quickly about the visions, the flashing and the woman running from her former haven; how she identified deeply with the woman. She told Dr. Boen that she felt so connected with the woman in the dream that it felt like it was she herself was running through the thorns, feeling the pain, the emptiness, the cold. She tried to convey the hopelessness, confusion and fear that she felt as they emanated from the couple in the dream but she wasn't sure how clearly she was communicating with Dr. Boen. She tried not to leave out a single detail. When she was finished, she was exhausted and out of breath.

Dr. Boen sat back in his chair, keeping his face neutral though his mind whirled with all the implications. He had always tried to present himself in a positive way, with a posture that showed interest and sincere concern for his clients, but right now his hands were tightly squeezing the pencil he had been scribbling notes with when Sarah was speaking.

Sarah noticed that the doctor appeared to be apprehensive, though he had said nothing during the entire narrative. She asked if there was anything wrong.

Dr. Boen was now caught between performing his duties as a counselor and letting his client deep into his life. His mind analyzed and weighed the possibilities, the pros and cons, as he tried to make a decision; one that could change everything.

Another bolt of lightning and an immediate boom of thunder rang out. They both looked intently into each other's eyes, experiencing a feeling of eeriness; something they couldn't quite define or explain.

Dr. Boen let out a slow exhale, put the pencil and pad on his desk, and sat back in his chair. He looked intently at Sarah and gave a slight smile as he prepared to let Sarah know of his dream.

~~~~~~~

Dr. Turgeon was meeting with his little local "think tank" as he liked to call it. He wanted to share his experience at Sue's school and specifically the questions asked by the students, especially Kelly's.

"Most of the questions were variations of the ones asked in the news conference," He began, addressing the group. "That made me think that the younger generation thinks no differently than the older generation."

He restated, "They may seem different, but in the end, there is not much difference."

They nodded in agreement, one counselor stating that his patients come to him with many of the same fundamental problems. "And I'll bet you that we are giving them the same answers that our predecessors gave their patients."

The Old Therapist sat in his usual easy chair taking in all that was being said. He felt that over his many years of counseling that he had observed the same things. His desire to find something different was overwhelming to him.

Dr. Turgeon then said that maybe they should not look for a difference but seek to find that scarlet thread of similarity that seems to run through humanity from generation to generation.

He then posed this question to the group; "If we were to look at the clients that we, collectively, have counseled over the years, and choose seven of those who moved on to flourish in life, what do you think would be the most consistent thing they embraced that made the difference? I mean, what was it that caused the change? Or conversely, what did they eliminate that made a difference?"

The group grew quiet for a moment, each gathering their own thoughts.

Then the discussion began. It took the group the better part of their morning together to answer. Each attendee shared different stories about different people. Most of the stories were similar; some a little different. As they all talked, The Old Therapist listened intently, making notes on an old, dog-eared writing tablet.

When they had finished sharing, Dr. Turgeon turned to The Old Therapist and asked if he would share what he had been writing and asked if he had gleaned anything significant from the discussion.

The group had learned well that years spent in their line of work should be respected and they had the utmost admiration for The Old Therapist. Even though he had years of experience, the old man made it clear to them that he, by no means, had "arrived" in this life or in his profession. He deeply esteemed those who had worked for years at their profession and equally respected those new in the field, for some brought a fresh way of thinking.

Time was running out and everybody realized this but wanted to hear from The Old Therapist. Dr. Turgeon had originally wanted to dig into some of his own recent experiences with the students at the lectures, but knew that he would have to wait. He felt this was good for him. He had learned that the phrase "In its time, for its purpose" was so applicable in so many ways; and now, especially.

The Old Therapist turned to the group and noted that time was dwindling. He said that he would like to take his notes home and look them over so he could better ascertain what had been shared.

"I will share this though." He said. "And we touched upon this a little the last time we were here. It appears that there are two common items that have been mentioned throughout our time today."

He made eye contact with every member of the group, then continued, "The first is fear. It seems that all those who sought our help had been held captive by some kind of fear." He let that sink in for a moment.

"The second thing is freedom, and this was common to those who went on to flourish in life. When I put these together," he continued, "it becomes obvious that those who have become free of their fears have become free indeed."

Dr. Turgeon's ears perked up at this. He wanted the whole session to begin with this and not end with it. But time was up and those there had obligations to meet.

He closed the meeting by suggesting that everybody hold fast The Old Therapist's words and consider them over the next week. He said that he hoped that they would be able to pick up where they left off the next time they met.

They all agreed and prepared to go their separate ways. The Old Therapist stayed for moment with Dr. Turgeon. He told him that he had recently received some of the unpublished writings of their mutual friend, Dr. Kawika.

"I'll bring them the next time we meet," he said.

Dr. Turgeon was ecstatic about the potential to review writings of a man he had respected so much, both as a colleague and a friend. He knew that Dr. Kawika had begun discovering things about the human psyche that were ground-breaking and yet ancient truths re-discovered.

They bid each a good day and The Old Therapist made his way home. Dr. Turgeon sat back in his chair on the porch of his home which overlooked his garden. His thoughts were interrupted by the telephone. The call was from Sue.

~~~~~~~

After meeting with Dr. Boen, Marc went directly to his office. He didn't like being late for meetings, and though he found them somewhat unproductive, he especially didn't like missing the daily ten minute stand-up meetings, the scrums. On this particular day, it happened that Chad was the "Scrum Master", and it was his responsibility to lead the team through the routine. Marc knew this and it was why he did not want to be late. Since the presentation, Marc had a newfound growing respect for Chad.

The scrum was uneventful. Marc and Chad lingered in the room afterwards to go over the next meeting; Marc would lead that one. When they were finished talking, Marc asked Chad if he was available for lunch. He wanted to talk to Chad about his personal observations and hopefully get some insight from Chad on things he was struggling with.

The two men had been able to spend some time together since Chad's daughter was born. Marc had taken the opportunity to tell Chad about the presentation and how well it went. He left no compliment unsaid regarding Chad's incredible presentation creation.

Still, Marc, always wanting to have the upper hand, wanted to know how to read people better. He was not only interested in how Chad was able to accurately anticipate so much from the attendees, he wanted to understand how Chad could be so mindful of people's interests. He just didn't understand how someone could be as intuitive about people as Chad was. Was this a skill that came naturally to Chad or had he developed it?

Chad was open for lunch and said he was glad for the opportunity to talk with Marc about some things as well. This unsettled Marc. Chad looked forward to talking with Marc at any level, but Marc was unable to think of a single reason Chad would want to talk to him. There was a great Korean café nearby and then agreed to meet there at noon.

~~~~~~~

Sarah sat back as Dr. Boen finished telling her about his dream and how it affected him. He said that because of the dream he started looking at the human condition and everything differently. He told her that it made him feel as though he'd seen the birth of guilt and shame and disillusion.

As he spoke, Sarah's breathing was short and her heart pounded inside her. She didn't know what to do or say. They were both caught in a moment of surrealism that transcended anything they had ever experienced. Sarah more so, because she now knew of two other people who had the same dream and she wondered, what if there are more? And what would the significance of that be? The thought was both exciting and frightening. She knew she had to tell him the very thing she'd been holding back.

As Dr. Boen looked out the window and watched the lightning put on a show of power, authority and splendor, Sarah inhaled deeply, then began to speak.

"The woman that was here the last time I came to see you?" she began. Dr. Boen looked at Sarah wondering why she would want to talk about Sue. "Well, I bumped into her this morning at a breakfast café. She was sitting at a booth alone and I was looking for a place to sit. She called me over to sit with her." She continued. Dr. Boen's expression was quizzical, wondering where this was leading.

Then Sarah told the doctor all about her meeting with Sue and how they discovered that each of them had the same dream.

Dr. Boen's eyes were open wide and he was completely dumbfounded. This time he could not hide his reaction. He didn't know what to think except that he now knew that the dream was so much more powerful and significant than he had ever thought possible.

They sat there in silence for what seemed like forever, looking at the storm outside and occasionally glancing at each other wondering how to even begin to talk about what was really going on.

~~~~~~~~

Marc and Chad ordered their lunch and then sat back and updated each other about their families. Marc was, as usual, impressed by how Chad was able to go into detail about the goings on in his family, something he was never able to do. This always made him feel like such a failure; beating himself up about this on so many occasions that is was almost commonplace.

Chad leaned forward and said, "It's a shame you couldn't make the dinner last week Marc. Everyone thought you did a great job on the presentation.

"Chad, I appreciate that, but I only presented what you created. I was just the delivery boy." Marc said, "As a matter of fact, I am glad I didn't go to the dinner, I don't think I could have handled the praise. " He gave a lopsided grin.

Chad raised his eyebrow and looked at Marc, wondering what he meant by the statement. He was about to say something along those lines when Marc continued:

"I was completely blown away by the contents of the presentation you prepared and can't fathom how in the world you accurately predicted every question from the participants."

Marc's tone became more serious, "All I did was follow your script, Chad." Marc paused before continuing on: "I want to know how you are able to read people like that. Have you always been able to do that?" Marc asked. He always thought that he could read people pretty well, yet he felt that Chad had something different; something more. And he wanted it.

Chad sat back in his chair as their lunch was delivered. He pondered Marc's questions and considered them at length. He knew that this was not just a question into some trade secret; it was more than that. Knowing that Marc had some deep internal struggles, he began to formulate an answer he hoped would allow Marc to open up.

They both sat for a few moments eating their lunch. The café was packed as usual and the air was filled with business people, blue and white collar, talking and eating and connecting. Chad always felt that meals were the best times to have conversations. He thought that both sharing a meal and making connections were both deep human needs; so necessary, so fulfilling. He paused from eating just to look around and simply take in the moment. Marc noticed this and observed a satisfied smile come across Chad's face.

"Quite the place, isn't it?" Marc said.

Chad nodded, "Yeah, it's awesome. Love the different people that come here."

"So, have you always been able to read people like that?" Marc asked, bringing the conversation back to the topic he wanted to discuss.

"First, you asked if I have always been able to read people the way I do." Chad looked directly at Marc before continuing. "Well, the easy answer is no, I have not. But, I have to say that it has always been there inside of me. I mean, I had never been able to tap into, or better yet, achieve the composure to be free from my thinking."

Marc jumped in saying, "You mean free "IN" your thinking, don't you?" Yet just as Marc said it, he felt he was wrong and added, "I take that back. I think you know what you are saying."

Chad looked at Marc, who had almost finished his meal. He was glad Marc corrected himself. He felt it gave him license to continue to speak very freely.

"Years ago," Chad began, "before I was married to Elise, I was living through some very dark days. It was so dark and I was so down that I even questioned my sanity."

Marc's face showed obvious disbelief. Chad, the eternal optimist? The guy who had it all together? Chad had days like that? Still, he said nothing; he respected Chad and did not try to minimize Chad's experience.

"Well, to make a very long story short, things began to change for me and my outlook on life when, within the span of about a month, I had three dreams that were so powerful and real, I had to take them very seriously."

At this, Marc sat up in his chair and began to feel like he was struggling to breathe.

"Dreams?" Marc asked. "Well, we all have dreams, and some very profound, but don't they usually pass with the day to day experiences in life and seem to fade away along with their importance?"

"I would normally say yes to that, Marc, but these didn't." Chad stated.

"Well, you have me now." Marc said, eager, yet somehow anxious about what Chad might say next.

Marc felt a cold sweat building in him; something inside, an intuition of some sort, made him know, before even asking, that what he was about to hear would impact him; he wasn't sure whether he really wanted to hear them or not. But he asked anyway, "What were they about?"

And at that moment, like an omen, a flash of lightning and roar of thunder filled the café and shook Marc to his bones.

Chad raised his head and looked around, studying the people in the cafe and how they all reacted to the storm. He had a smile that spoke of satisfaction, confirmation and peace.

"Why do you smile like that, Chad?" Marc asked.

Chad looked at Marc, still smiling and said, "Whenever there is thunder and lightning, I am reminded of the first dream."

Before Chad could go into detail, Marc asked: "Can you tell me about the dreams? Why did they have such an effect on you?"

"It's not so much what the dreams were about, Marc, as it is what I was able to glean from them." Chad answered.

Just then Marc's cell phone went off, interrupting the conversation. Marc had to answer, as it was their boss, Matthew, asking that they both return to the office. He told Marc on the phone that Harvey wanted to meet in two hours everyone needed to be there for it. He wanted to get together before the meeting to prepare for what he thought might be final negotiations. Marc sensed Matthew's excitement at potentially finalizing the terms of the merger at last.

Though the news was exciting and promising, Marc regretted having to end the luncheon with Chad. He wanted, even needed, to hear what Chad had to say. And now, he would have to wait.

As Marc got up from the table, Chad motioned that he sit for a moment. "Matthew can wait a few minutes, Marc." Chad assured him.

"There's a lot more I'd like to say," Chad began, "but seeing that we only have a short time, I will tell you this:"

Chad inhaled slightly and continued, "My dreams showed me that I had been a slave to an old way of thinking."

"A slave?" Marc asked.

"Yes, and so much a slave that I was unable to do or be anything other than who I had been up to that point. I had been a slave to an image I had been portraying; an image of who I thought I needed to be. Does that make sense?" he asked Marc.

Marc looked at Chad, a little confused, struggling to comprehend the statement, and said, "I'm not sure I get it. Are you saying that you had been trying to live out a life that was not yours but somebody else's?" Marc verbally stumbled over the question. For Marc the conversation was hitting home but didn't want to let on.

"So, did all the problems really end with the dreams? Marc asked with a sense of astonishment.

"No, things didn't change overnight. My old way of thinking began to change and with each change, the darkness I'd been living in began to lift."

There was silence for a moment.

"I'd love to continue this conversation," Chad said, "Let's do it soon. But we should go now, the Man's waiting for us." He grinned.

Marc nodded in agreement. He realized that it had only been seven days since the dream. Chad had had three dreams within a month; he wondered what the significance really was.

~~~~~~~

"Well, hello Sue. What a wonderful surprise! I'd know that pretty voice anywhere." Dr. Turgeon said as soon as he picked up the phone. Sue returned his greeting, always feeling wonderful at most anything the doctor said. His manner always uplifted her.

"And to what do I owe the honor of this call?" Dr. Turgeon continued.

Sue had been on his mind ever since he'd visited her school. He thought about the time with the students; Kelley's question and the short conversation he had with Sue before he left, about lies that people believe about themselves. However, it was the statement he made to the students about trusting love that seemed to capture his attention the most. He had always wondered where statements like that came from. He never considered himself to be that insightful, but that day he found himself making a very significant and profound statement. Those little bits of wisdom kept him believing that there was something else going on with humanity; something very deep and spiritual, yet very separate from religion.

Sue had learned that the doctor was scheduled to appear at another press conference which was to take place about sixty miles from her. She had planned to go to the conference, so she called the doctor to see how long he would be in the area and if it were possible for them to meet up privately.

The doctor was more than happy to set some time aside to meet with Sue, which absolutely delighted her. Now, more than ever, she wanted to share her dream experience with him. She wanted to tell him the woman in the dream had believed a lie about herself and that it had drastically changed her world. Is this the kind of "lie" that Dr. Turgeon talked about, she thought to herself. And what is this "truth" that sets you free? She hoped their conversation would shed some light on that.

They set a time to meet up for coffee near the conference center. She hung up the phone, excited about the chance to spend some time with him again.

~~~~~~~

Sarah broke the silence. "Dr. Boen?" She began inquisitively, "We now know that three people had the same exact dream. Do you think there are more?"

Dr. Boen sat back in his chair and pondered the question. He thought of the many people that had crossed his path since he had the dream seven days ago. He wondered who could be an intended target for the dream. Who could benefit most from it? He suddenly realized that most of his questions assumed that the dream had intention, and if it had intention, then it had purpose. But most of all, he realized that if the dream had intention and purpose, then it had to have a source; it had to come from somewhere. And that brought him to wondering about the source. It was this kind of thinking that overwhelmed him because it created more questions than answers.

Sarah sat waiting for an answer from the doctor. She felt strongly that there was more; that there was intention; that it was imperative to find out who else had the dream; that the dream was something that pushed the super-natural. She somehow knew that enlightenment and understanding was the ultimate intention. She didn't know how she knew, she just did.

Sarah was young and impressionable and her disposition lent itself to fantasy. Having the dream was one thing, but knowing that others had the exact same dream on the exact same night pushed her to question much of what she considered as the normal human experience.

The doctor turned his head from the window, faced Sarah and said in a simple and direct way, "Yes. I think there are more."

This brought a smile to Sarah's face. It meant more intrigue; more drama; more fantasy; more to life than what she had known to date.

"What makes you believe others have had the dream?" Sarah asked.

Dr. Boen heard Sarah's question. He felt challenged to keep the ordinary professional distance between him and this client; the dream tied them together in a different manner and he could not deny it; the relationship had changed.

He spoke, "Forgive me for taking so long to answer, it is a complex and intriguing situation."

She nodded in agreement.

"The reason I believe that others have had the dream is because if three have had it then there is intent to the dream. If there is intent, then yes, there must be others and they will show up when it is time."

Almost before he'd finished, she asked, "But if there is intent, then there must also be a source, right?"

Dr. Boen nodded and applauded her wisdom with a smile.

The doctor sat back. She smiled. Lightning lit up the room and thunder crashed the silence. The doctor looked out the window. Sarah turned to the window as well and thought that there was nothing quite like a good storm.

Chapter 10

Harvey showed up with his executive team and wasted no time getting down to business. He outlined the agreeable terms and conditions of the merger in his normal succinct manner.

When the meeting had finished, Harvey invited them all to a small banquet the following evening to celebrate the successful negotiations and their new relationship.

They all shook hands and concurred that the rest would be left in the hands of the lawyers.

Once everyone was gone, and only Matthew, Chad and Marc remained, Matthew let out an audible sigh and his smile showed how pleased he was with the outcome. He congratulated both Marc and Chad on a job well done. His sincerity showed.

After Matthew left the room, Chad turned to Marc and said "Why don't we go out and celebrate!"

So, they packed up and met at a nearby business club they were both members of. It offered a good bar atmosphere with some private areas for quiet conversation.

After getting a couple of drinks, they found a section of leather chairs and sat, both basking in the accomplishments of the past week.

Marc didn't care much for small talk and as quickly as he could, he steered the conversation back to the dreams, hoping to pick up where they left off at lunch.

"I want to go back to our conversation at lunch today." Marc started. "You said you'd had a few dreams that had a profound impact on you." Marc hesitated, wanting to admit he'd had an unusual dream too, but choosing to say nothing for the moment.

He looked directly at Chad, "I've always had an interest in dreams and their meanings. Can you tell me more about the dreams and why they impacted you in such an important way?"

Just then a flash of lightning lit up the sky and the room to such an extent that it stopped everybody from their drinks. The thunder that followed seemed to shake the very ground beneath them.

"Wow! That was awesome." Chad said.

Marc sat there motionless; the thunder cascaded him back to the dream, complete with the overwhelming feelings of fear, confusion and abandonment. It felt like he was falling off a precipice. He shook himself out of it as Chad began to speak.

"Every time there is lightning and thunder, I am thrown back to my first dream." Chad said. He began to describe his first dream and Marc sat there completely astounded and even a little fearful. As Chad continued to speak of the dream, Marc periodically responded with a nod or a word that eventually led Chad to believe that Marc had experienced something similar.

A curiosity rose up in Chad's mind. "Marc." he began. "Did you have a similar dream? I get the feeling that there is significance to some of the things you have asked and can only think that you have."

The waiter returned with Marc's drink and Chad requested his second round. As the waiter left, Marc looked at Chad wondering how to begin.

Simplicity seemed the only way: "I had the exact same dream." he said.

Chad sat back, unable to grasp the significance of this for the moment. The waiter brought his drink. Marc threw his second drink down and asked the waiter for a third.

Gradually, Chad grew a grin on his face that made Marc feel a little more at ease.

"I'm not surprised in the least that it would be you that also had the dream, Marc." Chad began.

"Really?" was Marc's reply. His curiosity was breaking down his defenses; he felt himself slip ever so slightly into a deeper realm, a realm that might possibly contain some of the answers he so needed.

Chad continued: "I have thought for some time now that more people have had the dreams and that these people were chosen, in a way; that there's a reason why we were given the dreams."

Marc wanted to know what the other dreams were, but guessed that Chad would not tell him. He knew that it would serve no purpose to have a "sneak preview".

"I told you that I had three dreams Marc." Chad began, as if reading his thoughts. "And now I believe that you will have three as well. I don't know if the next two will be the same as mine and I don't know when they will come, but I believe, just as sure as I am sitting here, that they will come."

Before Marc could say anything else, Chad asked him if he knew anyone else that also had the dream.

Marc sat back a moment and told him how his marriage counselor mentioned a dream in their session the other day. "I think he has." Marc said. Chad returned that same grin that intimated he was all too happy that he was not alone.

"You said that your dreams came to you within a month, right?" Marc asked.

"Yes. But I don't think there is any particular timing or way that the dreams will come. I just really believe that you will have more." Chad responded.

At that point, Matthew came through the entry, spotted the two guys and made his way to them with a huge smile on his face. "The office told me you would be here, and my appointment ended early, so I thought I would join you."

Chad and Marc looked at each and changed their whole composure and welcomed Matthew. The conversation switched to small talk, business talk and plans for the future. Nothing further was mentioned about the dreams; Chad was glad. He felt that Marc needed to experience the series of dreams alone and process them on his own, as he himself had done. For some strange reason, Marc felt the same.

~~~~~~~

Dr. Turgeon arrived at The Old Therapist's house early in the evening. The house was nestled in a small cove on a secluded lake. It had a rolling, well-manicured lawn that led down to a peaceful beach. The lake was pristine and flat mirroring Rattlesnake Mountain which stood majestically beyond the opposite shoreline. A dock stretched out on the left side of the beach and an old Chris Craft motor boat was tied to its side. The mahogany sides of the boat shimmered on the surface of the lake. The Old Therapist was especially fond of his boat and the home he had lived in for almost his entire life. He had grown up on the lake, and he and his wife had raised four children there. His memories were filled with all the sights and sounds of a serene, carefree youth that he promised to provide for his children. It was a gift given to him that he was so happy to have passed on to his children.

The Old Therapist welcomed Dr. Turgeon into his home. They walked out to the porch that looked out over the lake. He had recently opened up the porch for the summer months by taking down the windows and leaving the screens. It was a warm spring evening and the soft breeze whispered through the pine trees with a song that created an aura of comfort accented by the almost silent sound of the lake embracing the shore.

The sun had begun its descent over Rattlesnake and its reflection on the lake was only disturbed by an occasional ripple made by the loons that paddled past the house.

Dr. Turgeon turned to The Old Therapist as they settled in the Adirondack rockers that lined the porch and noted that the sights and sounds before him settled his mind.

"Places like this are a piece of heaven on Earth," he said to his friend.

The Old Therapist smiled and said that he could not imagine anybody coming here and not realizing the perfection of creation. Dr. Turgeon nodded in agreement and they both sat there for moment quietly letting the perfection envelop their beings.

Eventually The Old Therapist broke the silence by telling Dr. Turgeon that he had read the thesis a number of times and found it well written, insightful and thought provoking. He added that he also wondered what kind of response the general public would have to some of the statements that challenge the status quo. He even ventured to say that the culture he grew up in no longer exists, and that today's world appears to be more accepting of new ideologies. "The question," he said, "is 'What good will a new ideology do?'" After a pause he asked, "Will it change anything? Fix anything?"

They continued talking for a time about the thesis, sharing individual experiences with religions, cults and governments. In the end, agreeing that there was really no difference between them and that, in order to exist, all three need to control how people think. They also agreed that this kind of thinking made most people fearful and defensive, therefore perpetuating the age-old cultures which would never allow disclosure or, heaven forbid, change.

It was an ordinary conversation for them and The Old Therapist was happy for the company. To him life did not need to deliver stimulation through excitement. He was content in his life. His only regret, if you would call it an actual regret, is that he wished he had discovered this peace much earlier in life. This thought never stayed with him long. He felt that to dwell on it would rob him of the goodness he was living in now.

The Old Therapist then turned to Dr. Turgeon, and with a look of concern said, "Today is an anniversary day for you, isn't it?"

Dr. Turgeon lowered his voice with his head a little saying that it was two years ago today that his wife had passed away.

"I think you have an anniversary today also, yes?" Dr. Turgeon returned his question with an equal look of concern.

The Old Therapist nodded and smiled saying, "Yes. It has been ten years now that my wife died in that car accident."

It was a something they had in common, even though it was not a happy one.

Dr. Turgeon looked at his dear friend and couldn't help but see that his countenance had not fallen, but instead noticed a smile of serenity on his face.

"You seem to have adjusted very well in your life." Dr. Turgeon said. "It takes time doesn't it?"

The Old Therapist turned to Dr. Turgeon: "It takes more than just time," he shared, "In fact, I find that time doesn't always heal things properly."

"I think I know what you mean," Dr. Turgeon stated. "I find that in the two years since my wife's passing, life continues to present me with thoughts and regrets that challenge me and my sense of wellbeing."

The Old Therapist looked at Dr. Turgeon. He was thinking of a way to tell him that he had not experienced that in his life. He looked intently at Dr. Turgeon and with a most sincere and inquisitive look, said: "I'm going to ask you a question that you need to consider with all honesty and openness. You do not need to give me your answer. It is more important that you hear your own answer."

Dr. Turgeon's face was downcast even in the midst of so much of nature's beauty. "Okay," He said. "What's the question?"

As he gathered his thoughts, the old man leaned back in his Adirondack rocker and looked out at the pristine stillness of the lake with old Rattlesnake perfectly reflected on its surface.

"Years ago", he started "when my wife died, Dr. Kawika was the first person to visit this home. We sat here on the porch on a night much like the one we have now. He asked me this same question. I never gave him my answer. I didn't need to. I knew its intention, which began a wonderful healing experience from the tragedy I was living in." The Old Therapist paused to be sure he still had Dr. Turgeon's attention.

"On that night", he continued "our old friend turned to me and asked me what it felt like to be me. So, I am asking you the same question. What does it feel like to be you?"

Dr. Turgeon had been leaning forward in his chair, but as The Old Therapist delivered the question, he sat back and stared out at the lake. The fact that the question came from Dr. Kawika, caused him to take it very seriously. He had seen firsthand the impact it had had on The Old Therapist. Now the question was being posed to him.

The call of a loon shrilled out from a distance and echoed over the still waters of this piece of heaven on earth. And as Dr. Turgeon sat there pondering the question, he began to feel totally connected to all that existed. Tears welled up in his eyes and a smile of contentment appeared on his face. Minutes passed as Dr. Turgeon sat and watched the evening descend over the lake. He turned to The Old Therapist and tried a couple of times to speak, but stopped, considering what he wanted to say. He was trying to put together in his mind the truths from his heart. With a sudden insight, he realized how fruitless it was; that the mind was not capable of comprehending the depth of the human heart.

The Old Therapist sat there in his favorite chair, in his favorite place, pondering his favorite things. He had the aura of being at peace with all that existed, including himself. As Dr. Turgeon sat there on the porch, he found himself captivated by the moment in which they shared. His shoulders, began to relax. The pounding in his chest began to ease and he noticed his breathing slowed; he was calmed by the vista before him. He finally sat back, relaxed and relieved.

A loon called out again breaking the silence with an aria that seemed to be a psalm of worship. The Old Therapist turned to Dr. Turgeon and told him how his wife had loved her loons. He said that he had always heard them before, but that his wife helped him to love them. He added how grateful he was that so many things of beauty had been brought to his attention by his wife. "I will be forever grateful for those things and the many other gifts that she gave me in this life," he added.

"I think I understand," Dr. Turgeon said. "In fact, I know I understand."

The Old Therapist turned to Dr. Turgeon with a smile that could only be seen by angels and said, "I'm glad you came tonight."

They spent the rest of their time talking about the thesis. The Old Therapist commented on its structure and the way some points were delivered. He never suggested change to its content, just suggestions on how they can be heard.

The evening closed with them witnessing the stars duplicated on the mirrored surface of the lake.

The Second Dream Filled Night

Chapter 11

The man woke up to the sun piercing through the small opening of the cave. It took him a moment or two to realize where he was. The chill he felt over his body and the hardness of the place where he slept told him he was no longer in his garden home.

He looked over at the woman and she appeared still and asleep. He paused for a moment and the reality of this new life set in. He had always awakened to a warm sunny day filled with the aroma of a flora that stirred his senses and filled him with peace and contentment.

He felt hunger pangs and realized that food was not within an arm's reach; he was unaccustomed to this. He got up and looked outside the cave into a forest barren of fruit and vegetables. The hunger pangs grew. It was a feeling never felt before.

He felt pain in his legs and feet; another new sensation for him. Looking down, he saw that there were scratches and cuts on his bare legs. He noticed dried blood from a few of the deeper cuts and remembered running through the brush while searching for shelter the night before. He remembered how frightened they both were. And though the fear still lingered, he ventured out to find food for them.

The woman awoke to the stark knowledge of where she was, a place so foreign, so strange, she knew this was not her home.

She looked around and saw that her man was gone. Terror overwhelmed her and she wept a river of tears from fear, abandonment and the shame that had followed her out of the garden. Her mind tempted her with regret for the decision she'd made to follow him; why didn't she stay?

Just then, the man appeared at the entrance to the cave, his arms filled with fruit he had found after a lengthy search. She was still weeping uncontrollably. He stood at the entrance not knowing what to do. He had never seen her behave in such a way. He wanted to console her, but the thoughts of his betrayal overwhelmed him. He did not know if she would receive his comfort, but decided to go to her. He placed some fruit at her feet and sat near her, within arm's reach.

She lifted her head and saw that he had tended to her need for food. Silent, hot tears slid down her face as she threw her arms around him for comfort. He held her tightly and they sat there, together again, yet somehow so alone and unsure of what lay before them.

~~~~~~~

The piercing scream from the younger boy sent a bolt of terror through them and they froze, unable to move. The woman took off running first; the man followed and overtook her as they ran to the field where the boys had been working. When they arrived, the horror of the event stopped them in their tracks. The older son stood there, blood on his hands; the younger son lying there, bloodied, motionless, breathless, gone.

They ran to the side of the younger son lying on the ground. Shaking him and hoping beyond hope that he would show some signs of life; they quickly realized it was fruitless. His life's blood pooled into the very soil that gave them their blessed sustenance; he was dead.

They lifted their heads at the same time and looked upon the elder son, wondering why and how such a thing could have happened. Grief began to overwhelm them; accusation tempted their emotions.

The older boy watched them in their pain and bewilderment. He could think of nothing else but to run away. And he did; never to return.

The man and the woman watched him leave. He ran like a wild man, kicking up dust, and screaming in anguish. They called out to him to no avail. He too was gone and once again they were alone. They were overwhelmed with agony and despair, feeling once again the waves of guilt and shame that washed over them so often, ever since the very first night in the cave.

~~~~~~~

The crowd was relentless in their hysteria as the procession made its way to the place called "Skull". Bumping, jostling, shouting, each one seemingly in their own world, thinking only of their own position on the matter at hand.

The people were mixed in their response to the event. Some were cheering, wanting it to continue; others mourning in horror, grief stricken that this was actually happening.

The guards prodded and pushed the convicted ones to move on at a faster pace only to see one fall to the ground. Many in the crowd cheered all the louder at his pain.

They arrived at the appointed destination and the guards performed their horrific duty, positioning each convicted man to a place of complete helplessness, seemingly oblivious to the pain they inflicted and their assault upon the accused men.

After a time, the guards sat beneath the one who held most of the interest of the crowd. They took his garments and drew lots to see who would keep his clothing. The one hanging above them saw the spectacle all around him, his vantage point was grave yet vast. He lifted his eyes to the heavens and said, "Forgive them, for they know not what they are doing."

Just then the sky darkened, lightning flashed and thunder shook the ground. The crowd began to scatter but the mourners merely bowed their heads crying out "No! No!" as the lightning and thunder pounded the world around them, destroying any semblance of order and tearing their hearts to shreds.

Chapter 12

"No! No!" Marc and Sue both screamed simultaneously as the booming sound of thunder pierced their sleep. They sat up in bed; their hearts pounding. They both realized they had awoken with the same shout, the same breathless fear and assumed in astonishment, that they had both had the same dream.

Sue started to weep softly, saying, "No! No! Not another one.", as she covered her face with her hands, trying to slow down her breathing in an attempt to calm her terror.

Marc extended his arm around Sue to comfort her, but he was still stunned by his own dream and now, to add to it all, was Sue's comment about 'another one'.

"Another what?" Marc asked while trying to calm his own breathing and steady the pounding of his heart.

Sue brought herself under control and told Marc about her previous dream.

Marc sat there stunned.

Sue wept.

Marc gathered himself and told Sue all about his dream and they both sat there, silent, so wrapped up in their thoughts that the flash of lightning and the crash of thunder didn't seem to bother them like it had before.

He realized he was holding her and she didn't seem to mind.

"Talk to me, babe." he said, in a tone reminiscent of an earlier time in their relationship. She stopped crying and rested against him.

"It's the kids," she whispered, "the kids in the dream and our kids too."

He just held her and waited for her to continue, knowing there was more.

"I don't want to lose them," she said as another tear slid down her cheek.

"We're not going to lose them."

Sue asked, "How can you be so sure?

Marc held her tighter. "Because we love them. And I believe in love."

She was touched to hear these words come from him; it reminded her of the man she fell so deeply in love with years ago.

"Tonight we'll talk with them, okay, babe?" Marc said.

She smiled and rested her head against his chest.

~~~~~~~

On the other side of town, Sarah awoke to the crash of thunder crying "No! No!"

When she realized she had come out of a dream, she looked around to find that her husband had already left for work. It took her awhile to gather herself and in time she realized this was yet another dream that she would not forget. She thought of Sue and wondered immediately if Sue had had the dream also.

She slowly got out of bed and walked to her bedroom window. Gazing out at the tempest, her hands covering her womb, she looked at her calendar and realized she was more than two weeks late. "I can't believe that I might be pregnant" she muttered to herself. They hadn't been trying to get pregnant and yet they weren't taking steps to prevent it.

Though she really loved children, she was deathly afraid to be a mother. Her thoughts went to her teenage years and the responsibilities heaped on her in the care of her younger handicapped sister. Resentment welled up inside her and she wondered if she would resent the responsibilities of being a mother. She thought about the parents in her dream. She always believed that her dreams held a message. Had the guilt and shame carried by the parents in her dream been passed down to their children? Could that have somehow caused the catastrophe? And what would she pass down to her children?

Lightning lit up the room and through tears, she again repeated the words she woke up with, saying, "No! No!"

~~~~~~~

"Peter! Peter!" Dr. Boen's wife said, shaking him and trying to awaken him from the dream that was causing him to breathe so heavily. He seemed to be moving his arms like he was trying to hold back a crowd.

Dr. Boen sat up abruptly, panting, sweating, shaken.

He mumbled, "They didn't know what they were doing."

He looked at this wife, "Does anybody really know what they are doing?"

She shook her head, "What are you saying, Peter? I don't understand."

He simply dropped his head, calmed his breathing and looked at her saying, "You know, I don't think anybody in the whole world really knows what they're doing."

Dr. Boen turned to his wife, Angela, attempting to catch his breath as a cold sweat ran down his face.

Angela stared intently at him. She knew that he had another of his dreams and hoped that he would talk about it. Her look was easy to read and he began to tell her what was happening in his life and the dreams that had now become more than a professional fascination.

She was a passionate listener with a keen sense of understanding and discernment, yet she found it difficult to stay silent as her husband told her all the details of the dreams and the encounters with his clients.

He finally paused for a moment to consider again all that was happening. Angela seized the moment to tell him that her brother, Chad, had the same experience some time ago. She told him about Chad's dark days as she silently wondered if something extraordinary was happening in her husband's life as well.

Dr. Boen looked at his wife, considering her words, and remembered that Marc and Chad work for the same company.

Chapter 13

Hundreds of miles away, in the quaint seacoast town of Peaquod Pocket, Dr. Turgeon awoke to the distant sound of a blue jay singing a spring song announcing the birth of her newborn chicks.

He had been anticipating this day. Today, the group of professionals were meeting to listen to an unreleased writing of Dr. Kawika given to The Old Therapist by Dr. Kawika's wife, Josie. They were meeting at The Old Therapist's home by the lake, having breakfast together and then they would spend as long as was needed to discuss the writings of their much admired colleague.

Dr. Turgeon didn't waste any time preparing for his day. In no time he was on the road heading for that fabulous retreat by the lake, not far from the North Atlantic. He turned his radio on to the AM band and pressed scan, which he liked to do just to hear what different news and songs would cross his path as the automatic channel surf was on.

As he pulled into the driveway, his cell phone rang out an incoming call. It was Sue. He pulled into a parking spot and decided to answer the call.

"Hello Sue!" the doctor said in an inquisitive voice, wondering why she would be calling so early.

"Hello doctor. Do you have a moment to talk?" Sue asked.

"Why yes!" the doctor said noting that Sue's voice had an edge to it, a touch of anxiety.

They had already arranged to meet at the convention the next day. Sue told him that she wanted to bring a couple of people with her; that they had all experienced something quite astonishing and wanted to meet with him to discuss it.

The doctor was a little intrigued and asked Sue what it was that they had experienced. She told him of the dreams. As the doctor listened to her, he sat back in his seat and wondered. He had heard of this experience from Dr. Kawika. He assured Sue that they would meet and added that he might bring a colleague with him as well.

~~~~~~~

Dr. Turgeon took a seat near a window and everyone quieted as they turned their attention to the Old Therapist.

"When Josie, gave me this envelop," The Old Therapist started, "She told me that this particular writing is an unfinished work. She said that it had not gone through the editorial exercise and therefore was fragmented and included many side notes. She also told me that Dr. Kawika had tried to complete it prior to his death but was unable to."

He then opened the envelope for the first time, pulled out its contents and started with, "The title of this document is 'The Eden Virus'". He began to read.

From the time of my early teens, I began to question the intentions of the authorities in my life. It was not that I was a rebel at heart, but that too often in my early years, those authorities tried to lead me down paths that didn't make sense to me. Instead of equipping me to handle where life itself would take me, they would attempt to fill me with their own beliefs and expect me to accept them without question. I would later refer to this as expecting me to do the "goose step".

As time went on, I began to realize that when presented with ideologies that had no scientific foundation, I would need to use my imagination to find some way to accept the teaching. For example, to accept that a loving God existed, I needed to imagine what this God looked like, acted like and how He related to me and the world around me. And when faced with the concept of a cruel reality (disease, poverty or untimely death) or a fearful teaching (sin, the devil or hell) and the nature of this loving God, I needed to forego logic and accept it all blindly, convincing myself that I would not understand all that there is but some kind of reasonable explanation would await me at my death. It was also at this time that I began to ask what would most churches do if they did not have sin, the devil or hell as a part of their teaching.

I later found myself observing the many changes implemented by the major religious organizations, specifically the ones that that professed the Bible to be the "Word of God". Most notably were changes made by the Catholic and Episcopal churches. Things that would have been perceived as blasphemy some twenty years earlier, were now acceptable and commonplace. Where before, only men were allowed to administer the holy services, women were now allowed to do so. Where before, gays and lesbians were subject to excommunication, these people were not only allowed to practice the doctrines of the church, they were given places of authority within the church. These changes did not bother me in the slightest. What was most disturbing was that the changes were put into practice for the sake of accommodation and to meet the problem of diminishing numbers in the church; the holy rules, changed by people, to satisfy a secular concern or more obviously, a simple business decision.

It was around that time that I came to see that these religions always interpreted scripture to their benefit and never to their deficit. I can now apply that observation to all those religions who hold some sacred scripture as a final word of what God desires for "His people".

For reasons not even known to me, I began to notice how people are so easily convinced to believe anything if it is presented in the right manner at the right time. I thought of the influence of Hitler as he fortified his army with tens of thousands of German teens and young adults.

I even saw our own government convince the masses of a righteous reason to endanger the lives of hundreds of thousands of young American soldiers in the Vietnam War which would eventually take some 56,000 lives."

The Old Therapist paused and said, "There is a margin note to cross check this number. He wrote that it might more accurately be 46,000 lives."

Then he continued reading Dr. Kawika's words.

I have read or seen thousands of people blindly follow the likes of Jimmy Jones, David Koresh, Jim Bakker, Moon and others; many to mental and emotional prisons, many to their deaths, captive to their spiritual leaders.

In all of this, I ask "Why is the human psyche so susceptible to so much that they do not really know as truth? Why do we accept the words and beliefs of another without really searching for truth in our own spirit?"

The Old Therapist paused to read Dr. Kawika's scribbles in the margin. "He writes that these are only incomplete questions; that the real questions were eluding him at the time".

Once more he began reading the text.

These questions started in a simple form, but grew as time went on. And in that time, I obsessed more and more over why people are so affected by this weakness.

The answers to these questions came in small pieces. And as each piece came to me, I became more and more satisfied with my understandings. In the end, and it occurred about a year before I wrote this document, I had 2 profound dreams that directly related to my curious questions and observations. And it was the content of each dream that sent me to the Christian bible in search of the answers. This all brought me to the title of this document, "The Eden Virus".

In the first dream, I saw Adam and Eve the moment they were outside the Garden of Eden which directly followed their event with the serpent tempter.

As they stood outside the entrance to their garden home, everything was different and unknown. Lightning and thunder surrounded them and they experienced fear for the first time in their lives. Adam tried to return to Eden, but was denied entry by a large angel.

The most curious event happened next when Eve turned to enter the garden and the angel stepped aside to allow her entry. When I awoke from the dream, the first thing I did was research this particular event in my dream in every version of the Christian bible that I had. And in each version, only the man was sent out of the garden. It never occurred to me in the past to examine this most important piece of information. I had never heard it preached or talked about, but there it was. I was intrigued as to what this could mean and what its implications were to mankind.

But in the dream, Adam begins to run to find shelter from the tempest that surrounded them and Eve, forsaking her opportunity to re-enter the garden, turns and follows her man through a world of thistles and thorns to find shelter.

After their frightening travels through the new angry world, they found a cave in which they could escape from the storm but not their terrible situation. They sat in the cave apart from each other, despondent, unable to fathom all that had just occurred.

A week went by before the second dream occurred. In that time, I studied the story of Genesis with the thought that this story reveals more about man's condition today than I had ever considered.

The day before the second dream occurred, I had just received word from my doctor that my illness had worsened and that hope for recovery was dwindling. This only increased my desire to understand the first dream's meaning and document what I had come to understand.

The second dream, a three part dream, only added to my now passionate desire to understand what was being given to me; and I now believe this insight is truly a gift.

In the first part, I was brought back to the cave that Adam and Eve had spent the night in. Adam awoke first and immediately upon realizing where he was, set out to find food for him and his woman. It was this act of consideration for his woman that helped them overcome the separation they had incurred as a result of the accusations Adam made towards Eve. In the garden story, he had blamed the woman for his actions, while the woman admitted her foolishness, confessing that she was deceived by the serpent.

It was Eve's words that peaked my attention. As I re-read the story, it became clearly evident that Eve was fooled into believing that she was not good enough and the eating of the fruit would make her better than she was. For some unknown reason, Eve had a low sense of self-esteem. And when the tempter suggested a solution to her predicament, she believed it as truth and succumbed to the temptation. After seeing how Adam treated her when confronted by God, I could see how she might have this poor view of her self-worth.

This all made me ponder once again, how man is so weak and easily believes things that are not necessarily truth. I then considered how mankind today strives so hard to be better, and that, based on a standard of measure created by man in his weakness, never accepting that he is perfectly and wonderfully made. The proof of this I could easily see just by observing the ad campaigns by any number of companies selling cosmetics or material items deemed to enhance a position in society, be it a car, clothes or jewelry. Mankind, I thought, has made idols of sports figures, elected officials and popular musical artists. Our civilization has established a standard of measure that our children are raised to believe in, thus perpetuating the problem.

The second part of the dream found Adam and Eve alarmed by the death scream of their son, Abel, after he had been attacked by his brother Cain. Cain had seemingly been rejected by God because his offering to appease God had fallen short of its goal. And I wondered how we had developed this belief in the need to appease God. This did not fit my imagination of a God so loving and caring to all that existed. These altars and sacrifices were not found in the garden, so they must have been a creation of man in his desperate desire to find acceptance again with his creator. I concluded that this mentality was taught to the boys by their parents who had the burden of being responsible for the exile from their garden home.

The third part of the dream was most upsetting. The scene was the procession of Jesus being led to Golgotha for his execution. The crowds were polarized in their response to this horrible event; some rabidly calling for his death while others in total unbelief that this could happen to such a man that had done nothing but kindness to all those in need.

After searching the scripture for solid reasons for his condemnation, I found that his only fault was in his consistent attack on the religious leaders of the day. He continually called them out for their hypocritical lifestyles and their manipulation of the scriptures to their own benefit.

At the end of this dream scene, I saw the centurions dividing the clothes of Jesus and casting lots to see who would get to keep them. It was at this point that Jesus is quoted as saying, "Forgive them Father, for they know not what they are doing". I had always thought that this statement referred to the centurions and their actions, but now believe that Jesus was saying this about all mankind; that nobody then and no one today really knows what they are doing as it pertains to the grand scheme of things.

When I awoke from this, the second dream, I was left with a sense of astonishment as I could apply all that I saw in the dreams to all of mankind from his beginnings. It was then that I absolutely believed that the "original sin" as so many religions have called it was not disobedience, as they want you to believe, but that it was the rejection of who we are and what our purpose is. And this, I believe was the birth of what I have called 'The Eden Virus' which to me is evident today in all of mankind."

The Old Therapist stopped his reading for a moment to let it all set in with those in attendance. The room was quiet as everybody processed all that they just heard.

"Dr. Kawika was unable to finish this document as his sickness overcame him." The Old Therapist said. "Josie told me that before he passed he told her of a third dream he had, but was unable to inform her of its contents. He passed the next day."

One of the attendees, a woman in her sixties, suggested that copies be made, distributed and the contents revisited for next month's session. All those in attendance agreed and as they departed, expressed their gratitude to The Old Therapist for his reading and hospitality. Only Dr. Turgeon remained.

As the two sat together in the meeting room, Dr. Turgeon told The Old Therapist of Sue's phone call. He asked him to accompany him to the convention the next day saying, if possible, could he bring several copies of "The Eden Virus" with him.

"I think this is something Sue and her friends need to read for themselves. Don't you?" Dr. Turgeon said.

"Maybe the whole world needs to read it for themselves." replied the old gent.

They both smiled as a deep understanding passed between them.

The Last Dream

Chapter 14

The man grabbed the fruit from the woman's hand and flung it at the tempter, hitting it out of the tree. As they watched the tempter slither away injured and defeated, the woman turned to the man who took her face in his hands and softly kissed her, smiling and showing his love for her as she was.

"You are perfect in every way," he said looking deep into her eyes, touching her soul.

"And we have everything we need. Come!" he said.

He took her hand and led her away from this peaceful place; a place they knew they would return to again and again. In her thoughts she still wondered on the tempter's statement and though they succeeded over the tempter's ruse, a seed had been planted and now the challenge was to let it die.

As they walked away, they passed a gate guarded by a beautiful large angel who brandished a shining two-edged sword. She tried to look beyond the angel but could see nothing except the tail of the tempter as it left their garden home.

He had walked ahead and found a place in the sun and sat down. She turned away from the angel and walked toward him. She sat near him watching as he leaned forward to study a flower. He looked up at her and smiled into her eyes. She smiled and sighed a sigh of contentment with a sense that they knew exactly who they were and what they were doing.